Tap Out Sessions: Erotic Tales

A. Ward

Table of Content

Chapter 1

On Call

"Dr. Green, please report to your office. You have a patient requesting your immediate attention," a gentle yet familiar voice echoes out throughout the hospital.

My phone begins to buzz in my pocket, almost simultaneously as the alert relayed over the intercom system. Looking down at my Apple Watch, I noticed the time. It's 11:30 p.m., and the shift change process is happening within the security team. Spending a couple more moments checking in on my final patients before the lone break in my evening, I feel my phone buzzing once more.

I need you… NOW!

With a slight smirk on my face, I excuse myself from my patient's room and make my way down the hall towards my office. Upon entering, I notice you, and the sight is welcomed as you stand before me with your blouse unbuttoned, exposing yourself to me.

"How many times do I have to tell you that I cannot drop everything to come entertain your foolishness? I'm a professional and have a job to do," I mention, inching my way closer to you with every step of the way.

"Well, Dr. Green, I'm technically a patient of yours as well, and I needed some assistance."

Taking you into my arms, placing a gentle kiss upon your

lips, I play along with your game and proceed to allow you to continue.

"I've been having warm sensations and spasms between my thighs. They've been making me lose control of my senses all day," you mention as I tower over you, looking down into your hazel eyes.

"Hmmmmm… I see." Lifting your body from the ground, placing you on the top of my antique cherry oakwood desk, I gently spread your legs apart and begin to drop to my knees on the cold, tiled floor to get a better view of the area in question. "It looks like you've released quite a bit of fluid today. I'll need to check to make sure you're still able to produce the proper amount of fluids."

"Whatever you need to do, doctor. Just please make me feel the way I should."

"Undress completely. I need to be thorough in my work. I need to ensure that I eliminate all possible causes before I diagnose you with anything."

Standing to my feet, I assist you in removing your clothing. As each article of clothing falls to the floor, I get a good look at you to ensure that I'm not missing any obvious signs.

"Initial prognosis, you seem to be just fine, but I would like to dig deeper. Sometimes the problem resides deeper in the body, and the eyes aren't always able to catch it."

With you standing before me, naked, I gently place my hand around your neck and ease your body down flat against the wooded desktop. Time is of the essence as the examination process begins. Gently, I adjust your honey brown streaked hair to remove it from your face. Gazing into your eyes, I slowly work my fingers across your smooth, brown skin, tracing your red lips before allowing you to suck on the tip of my middle finger. Placing gentle kisses on your skin, I work my way down your body, stopping at your breasts, ensuring that they're warm to the touch.

I touch the tattoo of three doves between them before placing one in my mouth, sucking the nipple gently, while caressing and rubbing the other.

"Shit," I overhear you moan out.

With the proper reaction, I proceed to the next region of your body and continue my examination. Allowing my tongue to flow down your abdomen, closer to the region in question, I can hear you adjust your breathing. I gently blow the trail I just made with my tongue as I look up at you, watching me.

"Relax. Please don't be alarmed. This is standard procedure."

Adjusting my posture, I prepare to get a closer look at the area in question. I gently run my hands over both of your inner thighs to make sure that your sensation to touch is still intact. Without hesitation, I open the lips of your pretty, pink pussy to get a mental image of the before and after of my examination.

"Are you ready?"

"Mmhmm," you reply with a slight moan as you find pleasure in the contact that my tongue makes with your clitoris.

With two of my fingers, I penetrate the entrance of your pussy and stroke upwards, pulling my fingers back towards myself. Coupling that motion with my head between your legs, your moans and sighs echo throughout the silent room, introducing me to the next wave of fluid that your body is preparing to secrete. Applying pressure through suction with my lips, I allow my tongue to work like an agitator in a washer, spinning both clockwise and counterclockwise against your pearl. Your moment of glory is near as you place both of your hands on the back of my head, thrusting your plump pelvis into my face, before letting out a vicious exhale of passion. Your body goes into shock as you tremble.

Standing back to my feet, I look down at you, helpless, still not made whole and decide to take the examination further.

"Don't be alarmed. You're about to feel a sensation like no other, but I promise you once you get past the initial pain, the pressure becomes pleasurable."

Dropping my slacks to the ground, I take my position and ease the tip of my throbbing dick into you.

"Fuck," you moan out as you indeed feel the sudden surge of pain as my dick invades your walls.

With every slow, long, deep stroke, your pussy becomes more accepting of my hardened nature. My girth stretches your pussy to its limit as my stokes become more accurate, more deliberate in reaching the depth it needs to get a proper diagnosis. Lifting both of your legs, I adjust your position to test different sensations that you may feel. With both of your ankles in one of my hands and your legs placed against my torso, I stoke faster... harder... deeper into you, forcing your juices to escape out and drip off the edge of the desk.

"Please sir, DON'T STOP!"

Stopping is the furthest thing from my mind, but the way your screams are echoing, it's only a matter of time before security comes, asking questions. I feel your hand reach out, attempting to hold me back, but it's to no avail.

"Move your hand," I state, slapping it away.

I take it upon myself to continue pleasing you but with a shift in my approach and stroke. Slowly pulling my dick out until I can feel your lips gripping the head of my dick, I thrust myself back in quickly, holding my dick there for a moment, allowing the veins to throb against your walls. You're on the verge of drawing blood from my arms as you have your nails dug into both.

"Handle this dick. Let me get that fucking nut out of you."

I repeat the process several times over and watch the tears roll from your eyes as you place one hand over your mouth.

"That's it, baby. Let me drain that pussy. Cum on this dick. Don't stop until you get it all out."

As I continue stroking, ensuring that not a single drop is left in you, I release your ankle and feel the lifelessness of your legs. I wrap them around my waist as I grip yours. My focus is no longer on you and your diagnosis, but selfishly wanting to revive your pussy with my dick until I release in you.

"Please, don't stop. I can handle it. Give me all of you," you cry out as I push forward, stoking your pussy with all the passion, energy, and power I have left.

Within a moment's notice, I let out a growl as your punch into my chest from the depth I've accomplished in you. I release every ounce of my nut into you and lean down to kiss your lips. The two of us lock eyes, exchanging gasps, attempting to regain our composure.

KNOCK... KNOCK...

"Security... Doc, is everything ok?"

I quickly rush to pull my slacks back up and wipe any beads of sweat from my forehead.

"Yes, everything is fine. I'll be out in one second."

"I just wanted to make sure. They've been paging your cell for about thirty minutes now.

One of the patients is needing you. You're the only doctor on call this evening, and no one knew where you'd gone off too amid the security switch."

Walking over to the door, I gently crack it and thank the security officer for his time and information. As he walks off, I return my attention to you, watching you as you struggle to regain the strength in your legs to function properly. Picking up the clothing from the floor, I attempt to assist you in piecing your ensemble back together. Before you can get fully dressed, I gently place my hand beneath your chin, lifting your head to look into your eyes before kissing your lips once more.

"Same time tomorrow, nurse?" I question with a sardonic smirk.

"I'll politely pass," you respond with a chuckle and wink. "I'll be sore. Besides, tomorrow night I may need a dentist."

The two of us share a laugh and final kiss before we return to the floor. You finish getting your attire situated as we head for the door. As we approach it, I take one hand and open it; the other finds its way to your ass with a firm smack to it.

"Regardless of what type of doctor you need, you know I'm always on call."

Chapter 2

Showered Glass

As the shower starts, I watch as you sit on the edge of the tub, taking a hand towel gently blotting your glistening brown skin in an attempt to dry up the beads of sweat from the sexual workout we've just completed. In a daze, I just gaze upon your beauty, your prowess, grateful that you're mine, even if it's on a temporary basis.

My awkward stare is broken, as you part your lips to speak.

"Can I ask you a question, and please answer it honestly," you command with hesitation in your voice.

Without a second thought, I nod my head to acknowledge your request.

"Have you ever made a woman feel as good as you just made me feel?" you question nervously, anticipating the answer.

Clearing my throat as you look up at me from your seat, I can't help but to think about the number of women that have sat in the same spot, asking me the exact same question.

"The simple answer is no; however, I can't speak for how other women may have felt. Yes, I aim to please, but the difference between those women and you is me. I give you my passion, I give you my pain, I give you a part of me that they will never see. You get to see my vulnerabilities, insecurities, and weaknesses. So again, my answer is no. I've never given another woman the same pleasure of feeling as good as you do right now. I'm curious to understand your reasoning in asking."

"Curiosity... Jealousy... I simply wanted to know. I've never given a man so much control of my body. I've never felt the need to be used as much as I feel it when I'm with you. It's like you give me the right amount of pain, yet it's gentle. You feed my desires, yet I'm never satisfied. I always crave you more. You treat my body like an instrument, putting your hands in places and working me to make the sweetest sounds. I'm on a high when I'm with you, a plateau of pure bliss."

Taking you by the hands, I lead you over to the enclosed stand-up shower. From the steam filling the room as I open the glass door, the temperature is just right for the both of us. As I lead you in, I proceed to continue our conversation.

"That's a ton of emotions to process at one time. Is that why you were crying through the process?"

"No, that shit was hurting for a while," you respond. We share a moment of laughter before you get serious again. "In all honesty, yes, I felt like you were giving me a part of you. You've solidified my thoughts with your words tonight."

No further words are spoken as I pull your body closer to mine. The feeling of your warm embrace eases my mind, and I can tell that feeling is mutual from your end. As the steam from the shower's water covers the glass door, I take a lathered washcloth and begin washing over your divine shape. Standing behind you, I work my hands over your chest and slowly down your torso. Your breasts sit up on your chest so perfectly, and your nipples are aroused, allowing my hands to drive every curve and terrain of your body as we stand cradled together with my dick throbbing against your ass.

"Do you want me?" I ask seductively in your ear.

With a slight sigh, you turn your head towards me and kiss me as the water trickles over our bodies. You take my hand and work it down towards your pussy as you let out a vicious moan.

"Does that answer your question?" you reply, biting your bottom lip, working my hand over your clit.

With my free hand, I reach out for the shower head and aim it right over the top of your clitoris as we continue to play with it. Keeping your body close to me as you reach out, slapping your palm against the wall of the shower, I feel you thrust your body back, gently grinding against my now throbbing dick. The blood rushes quickly to my manhood as I prepare to give you another round of passion for the evening.

Listening to your moans intensify as you let out a slight giggle before climaxing from the shower head, you look back over your shoulder at me.

"Kiss me," you command.

I oblige as I return the shower head to its holster on the wall. Placing one of my hands on your back and the other on your torso to bend you over, you place both of your hands on the glass doors. Now that you're in the position I want you in, I take the hand that was on your torso and use it to stroke my dick up to its full capacity. Giving your ass a slight smack with my dick, I part your ass cheeks so that I can work my way into you.

"Fuck your bitch, daddy," you sigh out.

Your pussy is as tight as it could be. It snaps back to shape as quickly as it stretches.

"Please, daddy. I need to feel you in me."

As you begin to whine, growing impatient with me, your actions and movement become deliberate, thrusting your ass back onto my dick, forcing me into your warmness deeper than either of us expect.

"Shit, baby," I moan out, feeling you grip every vein in my dick.

As I begin working my dick in and out of you, building up to the stroke that you deserve, I feel you thrust yet again. You've put me in a position where I'm powerless. I brace myself by putting my back against the wall, allowing you to take all control.

You utilize the advantage you have by arching your back with your hands still against the glass door, pushing off like a launch pad. The harder you push, the deeper I go. I can feel my dick pressing against your cervix with every pump. Taking a grip of both of your hips, I help guide your movements.

Your moans have almost turned into muffled screams as you toss your hair side to side. The hot water continues to fall over us, but it feels nothing like you do inside. You continue to work my dick as if you're possessed.

I've given you the advantage long enough as you slowly begin to lose momentum from the pace at which you're going. Maneuvering my body, I remove my back from the wall and get into a slight squat. Gripping your waistline tighter as I pull your pussy back onto me repeatedly, I'm deep enough that I can damn near taste you. In this moment, I want nothing more than my dick to become a part of you.

You release the chilled scream you've been holding and slap the glass as you climax yet again. I feel your body's energy draining as you begin to shake and get weak.

"Get that ass back over here," I say to you as you try to get away from the punishment your pussy is taking.

"Daddy, I can't take it anymore. You got it all."

I couldn't care less about your words. I know your limits as I continue to stroke in and out of you.

"Fuck," you cry out, biting into your arm. "Shit...... Damn...... baby, I can't," you cry out, moaning, fighting for breath.

As your body gives me a different answer than your lips, I

continue my onslaught until I feel you recapture your strength. As you do, I release my dick from your grip and turn you around to look at me in the eye.

"So, you just gone do me like that?" you question, pushing my body back against the wall. You lock your hands in mine as you kiss me as roughly as you can.

With a slight smirk, I get my hands free, squatting down to pick your body up. As we lock eyes on one another, pelvis to pelvis, I grind slowly, anticipating the movement I plan to make in you. Placing your back against the glass door, my dick finds its way back home in your warm embrace. Working your body up and down on my shaft with your arms wrapped around my neck, I can tell you're enjoying every moment. Your juices flow and are pouring out like the water from the shower head. We continue making love for a while until I feel your nails digging into my skin.

"I'm cummin', oh shit, I'm cummin'," your voice vibrates out against the glass shower doors while your cum-filled pussy remains jam-packed with my dick. "Shit, daddy," you exaggerate, motioning for me to stop. I stop my stroke and return your feet to the shower floor. Your body is drained as you drop down to the floor.

"Oh shit, are you ok?" I ask, extending my arms out trying to catch you.

You sit there, half dead, with the water dripping over you. As you look up, I notice that look in your eye. I've seen it before. You adjust your vision and look at my dick as it remains fully erect before you.

"The fact that this motherfucker hasn't cum for me yet bothers me. I got to fix that."

You waste no time, taking me into your mouth, stroking me with both hands as you bob back and forth. As you work my dick like you're stroking a genies lamp, I feel myself on the verge of exploding. You get a taste of my precum and remove me from your mouth, stroking my nut all over your face and chest.

"FUCK!" I yell out.

Every fiber of my being seems to have left my body as you continue stoking me until even my soul leaves the tip of my dick. Looking down at you, I see that smirk and devious grin. We have no words to speak to one another; this is who we are.

Chapter 3

Drain and Repeat

The house is quiet as I enter the living room, placing my keys down on the glass top coffee table. I know that you're home because the aroma of your perfume lingers as I walk towards the bedroom. Checking each door in the hallway, I can't seem to find you, however.

"Bae!" I yell out for you, hoping to get a sense of where you are.

As I walk through your apartment, I hear a ruckus coming from the back of it. I place my hand on the handle of my pistol, just in case there's an issue I need to handle. I spot you dancing around with your AirPods in your ears. Placing my pistol onto the dining room table, I make my way through the kitchen towards your position in the laundry room. I take you in my arms, yet it spooks you as I do.

"Shit, boy," you scared me.

"No need to be scared, baby. Zaddy's home."

As you turn to greet me, I wrap my arms around you. I've missed you.

"I'm glad to see you, but you got here quick today. Is everything ok?" you question.

Shaking my head yes, I look down at the time on my Apple Watch. You're right. I generally don't make it to see you until later in the day. There's nothing special about the day, but the unexpected change in timing allows me to use the moment to my advantage.

"I just wanted to make sure I maximized my time with you. Is that a problem, sunshine?"

"Of course not," you respond, running your hand over your neck. "I am hot as hell. I need to get out of here for a minute."

As you attempt to walk out of the laundry room, you're met with rejection at the door.

"In a second, baby. Go ahead and take them clothes off so I can throw them in with the rest of this shit."

"It's ok, baby. I'll just wash it later. There's no need to add to the load."

Shaking my head no, I refuse to reason with you. "It won't make sense to wash two loads for one outfit. Just take it off and throw it in. Hell, you need to cool off anyway, right?"

As my words begin to make sense to you, I can see you thinking through what I've just said. You concede and place your clothing into the washer as you look at me up and down, noticing my attire before pointing towards the washer, giving me a slight smirk. Without a second thought, I remove my work clothes and place them in the washer with yours. As I do so, I feel you place both your hand and head on my back. I turn around to hold you and kiss your forehead gently.

"Are you ok?" I question.

"I'm better now that you're here, and I might just love the way you smell."

As the washer begins to start its process, so do you.

"Let's be spontaneous," you utter underneath a deceptive smile.

As I tower over you, I look down at you with curiosity, smiling.

"What you got in mind, lil' mama?"

With your hand placed against my stomach, you gently push me back against the wall before dropping down to your knees, servicing my dick. I let out a sigh of relief as I feel the warmth of your mouth taking me in.

"So that's how we gone play?" I ask through deep exhales of breath.

You look up with a mouth full of my dick, smiling, as you put one of her hands against my torso, gently scratching me with your acrylic nails.

"Got damn, girl."

I look down at you as you continue to look into my eyes. I can see my soul in the reflection of them as it starts to leave my body. You've gotten me to a point of no return as my erection hits the desired strength for your liking. Stopping your onslaught on my dick, you stand to your feet.

As your turn around, placing your chest against the glass top of the Samsung washer, you spread your ass so I can see the wet mess your pussy has made as it smiles for me.
 Without instruction or hesitation, I slide myself as deep as I please.

"Mmmmm," you moan out, feeling me pierce your nature.

Your embrace is warm, drenching, and tight as the desires of your body react to my intrusive being. Finding my stroke inside you, I feel your hands reach out to scratch my abdomen.

"Too deep, king. Baby, you're too deep."

Taking one of my hands, I guide your waistline back onto me while the other grips your hair, forcing you to look upwards toward the ceiling.

"There's no such thing as too deep. That's just your mind's way of telling your body that it's weak. Block that shit out and take me. Make yo' pussy adjust to me."

My words ring out as motivation to you as your pussy kicks into overdrive. Reaching forward, you get a grip of the top of the washer, holding onto it as I dig deeper into your body with every stroke. As your body continues to adjust to my nature, you begin thrusting your body back into mine, moaning, sighing, begging for more.

"I'm ready to cum, baby. Make me cum," you cry out, continuing to throw your ass back.

Releasing your waistline because you're now solely in control of your motion, I slap the top of your ass.

"Not yet. I'll let you know when you can come on daddy's dick."

I'm so deep in you, I can feel your orgasm building up against my dick. Your walls are closing in, preparing to unleash a hurricane against me. Swiftly, I eject my dick from your grip, watching you almost fall to the floor. Your legs are weak, and you haven't even hit your peak yet. You look into my eyes, and I see rage. I knew that fucking up your nut would anger you, and I needed to see that attitude in you.

I turn you around, wanting to watch my dick abandon your pussy of its juices. Lifting you up, putting you atop the washer, I waste no time in jamming my throbbing dick back into you. As the washer goes into its spin cycle, I place both of my forearms beneath your thighs, holding your legs up.

"You better fuck me, and don't you stop until I cum," you moan out as I begin to work my stroke forcefully.

"Damn, I missed this pussy, baby."

Gripping your nipple rings, you look down at our body parts

as they dance with one another. I watch you run your tongue over your lips.

"This pussy missed you too… shit…"

The onslaught of my penetration continues as I give you every bit of energy I have left in me.

"Fuck… I need to cum… Please, make me cum… May I cum, daddy, please?" you ask in distress as your pussy continues to swell around my dick.

"Not yet," I respond, working up a sweat from the work being put in.

I have you so distraught, you can't even formulate your thoughts correctly. You're stuttering through simple phrases, but it doesn't faze me or the command that I have over your body.

"Please, daddy," you cry out once more.

"Not… yet…" I strain.

Moments pass, and I've finally tapped into your next level as your sweet cries turn into angered whimpers under my control.

"Fuck you… FUCK YOU… FUCK ME… I… can't… hold it."

I'm in full blown attack mode, punishing your pussy like a raging bull, constantly striking its enemy.

"Cum on daddy dick, baby… Let that shit out… Drain that pussy for me!" Letting out a violent roar of my own, I feel my nut seeping out into you. "Arghhhhhh," I growl out, draining every ounce of fluid I have in me.

You dig your nails into my chest and neck, scratching my flesh, adding to the mural of scars you've already made on me.

"Fuck," I moan out as I stand before you, gasping for air.

Although shaking from the act, you keep your hands on my skin, gently strumming your fingers over my clenched jaws.

As I lift your body up from the washer and begin to walk you into your bedroom, I lay you down in the middle of the bed and stand at the foot of it. My dick begins to throb again as I overlook your smooth skin, glistening with beads of sweat.

"Round two?" I question, reaching out, stroking my dick with your juices still on it.

You look up at me and laugh. With that simple confirmation, I know that you're game. After all, you're the exact replica of me.

"I got you, baby. Just give me a couple minutes. I need to regroup."

You motion for me to join you in the bed, and I comply. You lay your head on my chest as I strum my fingers through your hair. You begin to trace the tattoo on my chest before you break your silence once more.

"Thank you, I needed that," you mention.

"Don't thank me; that was your spontaneous idea, remember?"

You smile and think back over the events that have just transpired.

"You know what? You're right, and it was yours to put them clothes in the washer, so go put 'em in the dryer. I'm going to be right here waiting on you when you get back."

"Fuck the clothes; they can wait."

The two of us share a laugh and prepare for round two.

Chapter 4

A Thug's Passion

We gotta make this move today, Ru. We need you on the block. This shit can't wait.

After reading the text, I toss my phone behind me. I sit at the edge of the bed, inhaling another lung full of smoke as I look up at you with conviction in my heart, knowing that what I must do can't be undone. There's a chance that I won't make it back home to you tonight. With you standing before me, I take my hands and slowly work them down your hips as Tank plays vividly in the background.

It's worse when I look at you, so I close my eyes. Trying to stay on cruise control between your thighs. It's slipping away from me, and I'm begging my body to hold on please. I wish it wasn't over, I wanna keep making love, I don't wanna give this feeling up, it's so good.

Placing my head against your abdomen, I can feel the tears falling from your eyes, dropping down onto the back of my neck. I take my lips and form slow, gentle movements across your skin.

You lift my head and look into my eyes as they, too, are filled with tears. We speak no words, yet our silence speaks volumes. You place a gentle kiss upon my lips and guide my hands between your thighs, knowing that this may be the last time you ever get to feel my warm touch.

Slowly and gently, I slide my hands between your peanut butter brown complected skin and red lace panties. The thoughts begin to run through your head, and that fear starts to set in. You try to push me away but can't. I remove my hands from your inner thighs and take both hands, placing them on your face.

"Stop. I'm still right here, alive and well. Don't take this moment away from us."

My words are warranted and hold truth behind them. I place my hands on your hips and gaze into your teary eyes as I slowly begin to work your red lace Victoria Secret panties off of you, revealing your freshly shaven pussy. My touch is warm against your chilled skin. You're still tense as I pull you closer to me. As you step out of the red lace, allowing it to hit the floor, I ease my massive hands over your physique, admiring your beauty. I take one hand and grip your ass while the other one gently chokes you. I slightly tilt my head and run my nose over your pussy.

The alcohol and weed set in as I find myself wanting to do nothing more but to taste you. The way your body clenches as I breathe gently over your skin makes me grip your ass tighter. You let out a sigh of anticipation as both legs start to tremble. You don't have a need to say much more, as your body speaks to me for you.

"Don't move, don't move, I'm right there. The way you move just ain't fair, and it feels so crazy, if I take another stroke, baby, you gone have to save me. I wish this wasn't over," I recite word for word with Tank as he cries out my exact sentiments.

"I fucking hate you," you cry out with a chilled moan, feeling my tongue gently stroke your pelvis.

In the blink of an eye, my face and your pussy are intertwined in a kiss as they become one with each other. Taking your hand, placing it on to the back of my head, you submerge me deeper into your love. Reaching beneath you, I take one of your legs, elevating it up over my shoulder so that I can ease my tongue into you and take a sip of your sweet nectar.

"Right there, baby. Shit, right there."

My fingers find their way into the depths of you as I curl them to latch on to your pelvic wall. As you feel my fingers carefully applying pressure inside you, I begin to suck on your pussy, using my tongue like a paddle against your clit.

"Slower, baby… That's it."

I look deep into your eyes and ease up the pace at which I'm motioning my tongue. I take the tip of it and spell *I'm sorry* in circles on your clit as your body starts to contract.

"Oh shit," you sigh out with your legs beginning to shiver.

With one more gentle suction, I feel a rush as your orgasmic juices flow freely down my chin and onto my legs. Releasing your leg from its mount on my shoulder, I place your body gently on my lap as you gather your composure. While digging your nails into my back gently, biting my shoulder, you wrap your arms around me and squeeze as tight as you can, not wanting to let me go.

"Please, don't go do this," you ask me in one last attempt to keep me home with you.

My mind is made, and the time has come for me to go. My phone vibrates on the bed behind us repeatedly, and that's your indicator that you must let me go.

"Promise me that you're going to make it back home."

I look at you as a man, as your man, broken, knowing that I can't make you that promise with what must be done.

"I love you," you state, crying on my shoulders, squeezing me one last time.

"I love you," I reply.

As we share one last embrace, my mind is flooded with negative thoughts. Every sin, all transgressions run through my head. I've done wrong by you when you've done nothing but right. Even if this isn't my night to leave this earth, I know that it's my last to be with you. Granted, you know my past and accept my flaws, I'm addicted to the streets and know that my wrongs will come back to haunt you. Sometimes love doesn't win, and this is one of those instances.

Chapter 5

The Ultimate Submission

"Look at me," I command, placing my hands beneath your chin, raising your head ever so slightly while keeping you in place on all fours. Staring deep into your hazel eyes, I find the trigger that I'm looking for within them.

"It's not that I want to punish you for your thoughts or actions, but I'd rather train you to think accordingly. When you walk out of this house from this point on, you're a reflection of me. The way you walk, the way you talk, the way you dress, should have a hint of me attached to it. Is that understood?"

Your submission is arousing as you shake your head yes, acknowledging my demands.

"I don't give a damn what happens from here forward with your other situations. I've given you the chance to walk away from me, from this, from us. Yet, you still being here shows me that you aren't quite done with me."

"No, I'm not," you uttered.

Running my fingers over your head, I place a kiss on your lips before walking around you.

"Is this what you want?" I question, gently spanking you.

"Yes," you sigh out.

With a swift swing of my hand, I tap your ass harder.

"Is this what you need?"

"Yes," you respond once more.

I remove my belt from my slacks and wrap it up into my clenched palm before striking your ass twice.

"Is this your desire?"

"Yes," you whimper, allowing the pain to take control of you.

"Shall we begin then?" I mention, dropping my belt, taking ahold of your restraints.

Taking the straps of the harness that holds you bound together in my clenched fist, I give them a firm tug to ensure that your body stays mounted in this position, exactly as I want it. Your chest is pinned down with your ass in the air. Both of your hands are at my disposal, freely hanging between your thighs, able to move only from the tension or slack that I give with these straps.

Reaching over, I grab a set of anal beads. I run them between the lips of your pussy to lubricate them before gently easing them into your ass. You sigh out with pleasure, and the fun for the both of us begins. Reaching over once more, I grab a vibrating bullet, placing it in between both of your hands.

"Don't let it go," I instruct, forcing you to keep it in the grasp of your fingertips.

With one hand, I gently tug on the ropes of the harness, forcing your hands upward, teasing your clit while pulling the string of the anal beads to tickle your insides.

"Please fuck me," you begin an impatient whimper.

Adjusting the speed setting on the bullet to low, I began asserting my authority.

"We've played by your rules. Now it's my time."

I wrapped the straps over once more in my hands, forcing your hands upward, but this time, keeping them in place. The bullet is just in reach to gently tease your clit.

"Shit," you moan out in a faint cry as the sensation becomes unbearable. "Please fuck me."

With the light from the sun, which is piercing through the window and glistening against the secreted wetness seeping between your thighs, I spread your pussy, allowing my tongue to taste your divine feminine energy.

"I think someone's enjoying this."

My dick begins to throb effortlessly as I prepare to fuck you relentlessly, leaving my imprint on your life permanently.

"Understand that I don't do intimacy; I don't do romance. What I do is obedience, and as long as this pussy is under my command, you will obey me. Is that understood?"

"Yes sir," you mumble, biting into the bed sheets beneath you as you feel the head of my dick slowly stretching your pussy.

Tapping the head of my dick against your clit, I position myself and widen your stance, forcing a deeper arch to your back while keeping your hands where I need them. Entering you slowly, I can feel your flooded pussy grip my dick. With each stroke, I feel your disobedient nature succumbing to my ways. Every thrust is as powerful as the one before it. Your once death grip tight pussy becomes more accepting to my fully erect dick. As I work in and out, I feel the anal beads pressing against your insides, rubbing against my shaft inside you. Your body is loving the sensations as it rewards me through your long moans and echoing sighs.

As your pussy begins to contract, I know that at any moment, you're going to release yourself on me. I slow my stroke down, placing both of my hands on your ass cheeks, spreading them to watch my dick glide in and out of your wetness. Your cream covers every inch of me up to my pelvis, and your grip is so tight, it forces every vein in my dick out of hiding.

It's been a minute since I've had a woman be able to take all of my dick, but with every stroke, I feel your pussy allowing me to go deeper. As my balls slap against your hand, it forces the bullet to vibrate stronger against your clit. It fascinates me to watch you release yourself over my dick. The wider I spread you ass cheeks, the more pressure is applied to your clit, and your anal canal squeezes the anal beads tighter.

By accident your hand increases the speed of the bullet, causing a torrential downpour over my dick. You tremble and shake but never allow your love muscles to release the death hold it has on my dick or the beads. Your arch deepens further as your body becomes sensitive to my touch, yet, there's nothing more you want but to feel me destroy the remainder of your insides.

"Don't stop. I'm not done."

You look back at me, smirking, biting back down into the covers. You've conceded your defeat and now realize the error in your ways. Your body is now mine, and every sexual thought you have, will tie you back to this evening.

Pulling the anal beads from our ass, I force my dick in as deep as you will allow and release myself into you. I pull the rope of the harness upward to ensure that the bullet remains engaged with your clit. You begin to let out a barrage of curse words as your cum starts to mix with mine.

You've been fucked and possibly fucked well, but you will never forget the day and way my dick unlocked your new normal. On paper, you may be tied to another, but your mind, body, heart, and spirit now all reflect me and who it is you really want to be, which is my submissive little bitch.

Chapter 6

Crazy Love

After the conversation with my friends take a turn for the worse, so does your demeanor. A simple phrase sends you into a rage. I don't notice the disrespect in the moment, which makes you even more angry, as every second passes that I don't acknowledge your feelings. You look over at me with an evil glare, as I look back at you, attempting to figure out why the sudden change in you. You get up from our bed, and I attempt to reach out for you.

"Come here, you pretty girl," I say to you as you walk around the house with an attitude.

"Fuck you, nigga," is your response as you roll your eyes.

Your word choice pisses me off slightly.

"You fucking heard me. Get the fuck over here. Don't start this stupid shit today."

Raising your hand, exposing your middle finger to me, you walk out of the bedroom and head down the hallway. I remain seated on the bed, with my back against the headboard, smoking my blunt.

Not long after you exit, I hear a disturbance in the kitchen and what sounds like dishes breaking against the wall and floor. Breaking my peace, I get up from the bed and walk towards the noise.

"I hate you. I fucking hate you," I hear you yelling as I approach.

I notice the mess surrounding your bare feet and approach with caution.

"Don't fucking touch me," you state, drawing a knife from the drawer.

"Put the knife down. Let's talk this out."

"Talk? Did you want to talk when you were on the phone, embarrassing me to your friends? They don't have to know everything about our business. They don't have to know that I have an issue."

I place my blunt down on the counter of the kitchen and place my hands up to the sky as I walk over to you.

"I've told you. It wasn't anything malicious. I needed to vent. I just so happened to say the wrong things at the wrong time. With the way you're acting right now, however, everything is fucking warranted. Besides, they thought nothing of it, and they still love you like a sister; that's on my life. Now put the knife down."

"No nigga, back the fuck up."

You swipe at me, not wanting to touch me with the knife but giving me the warning that you're serious.

"Just leave. I don't want to do this with you today. You've already done enough damage, just go."

My refusal is apparent as I continue to try to walk towards you with my hands out to my side.

"I wasn't trying to embarrass you, baby, and I don't want you to hurt yourself. Please put the knife down."

My words strike a nerve in you as I watch you take your eyes off me, looking towards the knife in your hands. You begin walking through the shattered glass, towards the entrance of the kitchen, where I'm standing. Slowly, I pace backwards to not trigger any sudden movements. You hold the knife out in front of me, motioning for me to walk backwards. I follow your lead and do exactly as you want, attempting to not upset you further.

"Your boys ain't here to save you. Since you feel it's appropriate to bring me up, we'll see if they miss yo' ass when you're gone."

"Please put the knife down. You're taking a joke way too far."

You slightly laugh, as you punch the wall with the knife.

"Too far? The shit should've never been made, but it's ok. I'm going to show you exactly who I don't get to be. I try my best to do what everyone else wants me to do to control the animal inside.

I reach out, attempting to catch your hand, but you swipe and cut the top of mine. As we end up back in our bedroom, I stumble over a shoe and fall onto the bed. You hover over me with the knife and debate for a second if taking my life is worth it. Deciding that's not the course of action you want to take, you make a different decision.

"You say that you'll love me through whatever, right? That's the shit you told your boys. Prove it. Fuck me while I'm like this. Fuck me while I'm having one of my moments."

"I love you, but I'm not going to do that."

"Just like I thought, you're a pussy. You only love me when it's convenient for you to love me. When I'm normal. You can't handle the real me."

I have no words as I stare at you.

"It's either you're going to fuck me, or you're going to watch me fuck myself."

As you stab the knife into our king size mattress, you walk

over to my side of the bed and reach into my nightstand.

"Put my gun back," I state to you.

As you examine the .45 caliber revolver, I notice the twitch in your eye. You open the revolving chamber to see if it's loaded, and it is. You remove all but one bullet.

"So we're going to play a game," you state, walking back around to the foot of the bed. "You're going to sit there and watch me fuck myself with this gun. Every minute that goes by without your dick in me, I'll pull the trigger. You're either going to fuck me like I asked or lose me. The choice is yours."

Not believing that you would be seriously willing to take your own life into your hands over some dick, I play the game with you. I sit back, watching you shove the barrel of the gun into your mouth to lubricate it before guiding it into yourself. My demeanor swiftly changes as the thought of this being a game changes into a reality.

"Don't do this shit," I beg as the first minute passes.

Click... You pull the trigger, and nothing happens.

"Instead of fucking the woman you claim to love, you'd rather watch me give this pussy to a steel contraption. Suit yourself. Fuck," you sigh out as you begin to slide the barrel deeper into yourself.

Click... Once more, you pull the trigger, and nothing's happened.

"Only four chances left," you state. "I'm ready, are you?"

As you begin to slam the gun faster and deeper into yourself, I sit up from my position, torn about the decision I have to make.

The gun begins giving you a sensation, and the thrill seeker in you enjoys every moment. Your juices begin to run down the barrel of the gun as you prepare to pull the trigger once more.

Click... I take a sigh of relief as the gun doesn't explode in you.

"Ok, fuck! You've proven your point. I'll do it. Just please stop."

You look at me with a smirk on your face as you remove the gun from your pussy, dripping in your juices.

"That's a good boy. Now get him up."

I do as you command and remove my boxers, stroking my dick. My dick isn't giving you the response you're wanting, so you take matters into your own hands as you draw closer to me.

"It doesn't look like he's happy to see me like this. Does the crazy mama not turn you on, big fella?" you ask, talking to him.

Taking my manhood into your free hand, you begin stroking me up to your liking while placing the gun at my forehead.

"Is that necessary?" I question.

"Is that necessary?" you mock. "Yes, it's necessary. This is what I want, not you. I'm in control right now — not you, not my meds, not the fucking doctors. For once, this is me being me."

"It's rather hard to get aroused with a pistol pointed at my frontal lobe, but you couldn't care less." You spit into your hand while looking me in my eyes and ensure that my dick gets hard. As it unwillingly grows in your hand, you become pleased. You mount my lap, sliding me into the wet mess you've created.

"Hey there, big fella. Mama likes."

Taking the barrel of the gun, you slide it back into your mouth, tasting your juices off of it as you bounce up and down on my dick.

"Fuck," I state uncomfortably, allowing you to have your way with me.

Reaching out, you take your free hand and grab mine, elevating it to wrap it around your neck. As I gently squeeze, you become overstimulated and begin to cum over my dick. You force the barrel of the gun down deeper, gagging yourself to intensify your body's urge to release.

As you come off the orgasmic high you're on, you dismount me. My dick is flooded with your juices and still standing strong. You place my pistol back on my nightstand, walk into our bathroom, and grab a washcloth before returning and tossing it to me. You removed the knife that you stuck into our mattress and let out a small chuckle.

"Clean yourself up," you command, adjusting your hair by pushing it up into a messy bun before walking out of the room. "I'm going to clean the mess I made in the kitchen. You want something to eat while I'm in here? I'm sure you've worked up an appetite."

Just like that, in the blink of an eye, your personality has shifted back to one of innocence, of solidarity. Dumbfounded, I have no response. I have no words for the events that've just transpired, but this is the real you. This is who you are. Regardless of your condition, I love you in spite of, even if it kills me.

Chapter 7

Still Your Best

As I sit around, talking shit with my best friends, watching them play NBA2K 22, I hear a faint knock on my front door.

"Pause that shit for me really quick. Did y'all hear that?" Making my way over to the window to look out of it, I don't see anything. I approach the front door and open it cautiously. That's when I notice you bundled up in your coat with an umbrella. Your presence is shocking to me and quite honestly, alarming to say the least.

"Hell nah! What the fuck are you on? You've got a restraining order against me, and you pop up to my spot. What kind of fuck shit is this? Get the fuck on, man, for real. You can't be here. I've got company right now, and you making my spot hot. You got to bounce."

Your deep, dark brown eyes tell me that something is wrong. The redness surrounding your pupils is a dead giveaway. The fact that you've shown up to my house unannounced without giving a call, text, or warning in the pouring rain lets me know that you're fighting something. Regardless of our past or present, I still have a soft spot for you, and I hate it.

"I don't have anywhere else to go. I'm sorry. I'll leave," you respond through a cracking voice, becoming visibly upset.

Watching you walk away doesn't sit well with me.

"Fuck!" I yell out as I punch my fist into my palm.

Noticing that the storm is beginning to pick up its momentum, I reach out, grasping your arm, pulling you back towards the door.

"Get the fuck back over here, man. Come in. You got until the storm is over and that's it. I can't play this game with you tonight, on some real shit."

Without hesitation, I allow you into my apartment, sheltering you from the storm that's raging outside the door. The two of us walk past my friends, towards my bedroom as they sit on the couch just as shocked to see you as I am.

"Is that who I think it is?" one of them says to the others.

As they chatter, I escort you into my bedroom, a room that was once yours as well.

"Fuck...," I mumble under my breath.

Noticing that you're completely drenched from the rain and headed towards my bed, I reach into my drawer, grabbing one of my T-shirts, handing it to you.

"Don't sit your wet ass on my bed!" I yell out as you begin to squat towards it.

Beginning to pace the room, I contemplate on what to do and how to handle you.

"Alright look, get yourself situated. I'm going to get them out of here because it's apparent some shit ain't right with you, and I need to find out what kind of sick shit you have going on right now."

Making my way back into the living room, I walk over to the PlayStation 5 and power it off.

"Come on, man. You about to do this shit for real, dawg, all because she showed up?"

"This nigga here, man. She got this nigga pussy whipped."

My ears are met with a cascade of disappointing, yet obscene statements from my friends as I escort them towards the door.

"Y'all ain't got to go, but y'all have got to get the fuck up out of here," I say to them as they file out of the door, one by one, into the storm.

"I hope you know what you're doing, man. If she calls the police on your ass, don't call us to come get you," one of my homeboys mentions, walking out of the door.

As they leave, my curiosity sparks, trying to understand why you've driven thirty plus minutes across town to see me in the pouring down rain. As your ex, it perplexes me. Entering back into my bedroom, I notice the pile of wet clothes at the foot of my bed and you beneath my satin sheets, crying. Picking the clothes up from the floor and preparing to take them to the laundry room to dry them for you, I can't help but look at you, reminiscing on the way things used to be. Looking at you in the exact spot you're laying in right now brings back so many memories of when my life was at its most peaceful. You notice me watching you, and for the first time of the evening, I see that gorgeous, white smile of yours. You motion for me, and I don't hesitate to draw near you.

"So, are you going to tell me what's up?" I question as I sit on the edge of the bed closest to you. "It's pouring down raining, and most normal people would be in the house right now, instead of their ex's bed."

We both share a moment of laughter before the conversation returns to a serious nature.

"I just need you. I realize that the grass isn't always greener, and for that I apologize. I was in a very bad head space when I left here. I didn't realize how much it would hurt not being able to talk to my best friend."

Your words hit home and touch a place in my heart that I was for sure had hardened. There are still several unanswered questions that I want to ask, but I find it best to let them rest. Having you here, hearing those words, makes me not want to ruin the moment. Locking eyes with you, I lean in and kiss you ever so gently. You embrace my kiss and match it.

Abruptly pulling away, you get up from the bed.

"I'll be right back."

You rush into the bathroom, and I hear my shower come on. I begin to laugh because of the audacity you have. I clearly stated you can stay until the storm is over, yet you've gotten completely comfortable laying in my bed, now showering.

As you return from the bathroom, tying your hair up with the satin cloth I've held onto since you left, I can't help but to stare at your body in amazement. Your curves still form perfection. Although you've always been self-conscious about your fupa, it's one of the features that attract me the most. As you make your way closer, I can see your intentions in your eyes. Like a deer caught in headlights, I find myself stuck. Like any man in Medusa's gaze, I look into your eyes as you wrap both of your arms around my neck before mounting my lap.

"We can't do this," I state to you with reasonable concern.

Your actions show me that you couldn't care less for my words, as you place your warm lips upon mine.

"That's your problem. You fear what we can't do. Nobody is here but us. Let's take advantage of what we can do."

You tilt my head and begin to lick and suck my neck gently as I reach out and run my hand over your body, working down your frame until I grip your ass. You sigh and suction harder on my neck like a vampire drawing blood from its victim. Your body begins craving me as you push my head with your fingers, forcing my body to fall back on the bed. Repositioning yourself, you begin unbuckling my jeans. Your warm touch against my dick instantly brings it to life.

"I missed you," I overhear you state to my dick as you begin to stroke it up to its full potential.

With every downward stroke, I feel myself extending, growing at your touch.

"It looks like you've missed me too."

You are, in fact, correct. I haven't had a woman be aggressive with me in some time, and with you, it's always the same. You know what you want, and you take it. Now that I'm at full strength, you rotate your body, placing both of your legs on the side of me as you cautiously sit down on the head of my dick.

I can tell that your new situation hasn't been pleasing you. You're sensitive and tight, like a virgin. I place my hands on your ass cheeks, giving them a gentle massage, before spreading them to watch your stickiness leave a trail over my dick like a snail.

As you get comfortable, finding your rhythm, my hands gravitate towards your hips as I grip them, firmly pulling you down onto my dick. At the pace you're bouncing, I know that I won't last long. I reach out and take a handful of your hair as you continue bouncing like a rider at the Kentucky Derby.

"Slow down, baby," I moan.

You do as you're told and begin grinding in a circular motion. My dick is at its breaking point, as I'm pressed against your G-spot. Your pussy is creamy, warm, and hugging my dick like a glove.

"Fuck, I can't take this shit anymore," I mention through a clenched mouth.

You lean forward, grabbing my ankles, beginning to bounce your ass repeatedly on my dick. Your compliance runs thin as you decide to move at your own pace.

"I'm about to nut, baby!" I yell out. "Fuck!"

Releasing your hips, I grip the sheets of my bed as my toes curl, and I release every seed I have within me.

You aren't done and want more from me as you keep me locked into you, constricting my dick tightly as you look back at me devilishly.

"You aren't tapping out already, are you?"

"Hell nah."

My competitive nature kicks in as I see the desire you have. I begin lifting you up and down on my dick, allowing your pussy to stretch me back out as you grip me through every stroke. You reach down and begin to play with your clit, which makes your pussy convulse. I'm beginning to grow stronger in you again as you work to please yourself.

As you sit upwards to get a better feel of yourself, I wrap one arm around you, placing my hand on top of yours against your clit, lifting you up slowly and gently back down. While placing kisses on your back, I take my other hand and grip your throat.

"That's it, daddy. Right there, stay right there."

Guiding your rhythm and choking you is intensifying your sensation.

"Did you miss this dick?" I question.

"Fuck yes, baby," you respond.

"You bringing yo' ass back home?

"Yes, daddy."

"Cum on daddy's dick then, baby. It's all yours!"

Without warning, you take a deep breath before letting out the sweetest scream a man could hear. Your cream floods my pelvis as you've reached your destination. Taking my tongue, I lick up your spine, causing the hairs on your back to stand up.

"Fuck!" you yell out, slapping your hands onto your thighs.

Ejecting my dick, you lay back onto me, turning your body to place your head on my chest.

"I'm ready to come back home," you state, circling my nipples.

I don't have a response, nor do I want one at the moment. Despite the legal hurdles that we'll have to face in order for that to happen, I'm glad you've come back to me because we both know that I'm still your best.

Chapter 8

My Brother's Keeper

As my best friend and I make our rounds through the club, a sparkle caught the eye of both of us.

"Do you see what I see?" I ask him, looking in the direction of the diamond-like shimmer that bounces off the light in the room.

"You know I do," he replies.

The two of us walk closer to the distraction, and what we witness before us doesn't disappoint.

In a rhythmic cadence, the two of us take turns acknowledging the beauty that sits before us.

"They say the blacker the berry…"

"…the sweeter the juice."

"If it looks like candy…"

"…it's gotta taste like it too."

Our tactic works as we get a full-blown smile to show on your face. Although we've slightly embarrassed you by our corny exhibition, you're flattered.

"How are you doing this evening, gorgeous? My name is Ares," I mention.

As you extend your hand to meet mine, I gently kiss it, acknowledging your grace.

"And who's your silent friend?" you question with a smirk,

examining his six-foot, six-inch dark chocolate frame.

"This is my brother from another mother, Zeus," I reply.

He reaches out for your other hand and follows up with a kiss of his own to it.

"Can he not talk? Can you not talk?" you question him.

"It's a pleasure to meet you," he states in a low baritone tune, looking down into your deep, brown eyes.

Clearing your throat, you exhale a breath of air.

"Shit.... I guess you can speak. That was cute. So, what are ya'll, some type of spoken word group?"

The two of us look at each other and laugh. In unison, we shake our heads no.

"Not at all, sweetheart. We're just two young men who happened to notice the only diamond in this building. This is literally my brother from another mother, and we both happened to catch a glimpse of you from across the room," Zeus exclaims.

"Exactly what he said, beautiful. It was hard to miss that beautiful smile of yours and the rest of those your features," I make a mention, admiring you. "Besides, you're arguably the baddest thing walking through this club tonight."

"Arguably?" you bark, taking offense.

"Nah, not arguably. There isn't a doubt about it. So, what do we have the pleasure of calling this queen?"

You look at the two of us from head to toe, examining our footwear and attire.

"My name is Patience."

"Patience.... I like that," Zeus replies, showing off his pearly white smile.

"Ms. Patience, it's truly a pleasure to meet you."

Motioning for the bartender, I order another round for you to indulge in.

"Whatever you're sipping on for the rest of the night, is on us," I mention, preparing to walk away.

"Y'all walked all the way over here and are already going to leave? Typical niggas."

Taking your glass and turning it up, you snarl at us. The two of us look at one other with a raised brow before sitting in the two empty seats next to you. As the song changes, so does our conversation, as we dive head first into getting to know more about you.

"So, Ares and Zeus? How the hell did y'all get them names?"

"That's a question you've got to ask our parents. They were best friends and decided that's what they wanted to name us.

"Interesting. The God of Thunder and the God of War. So, tell me, fellas, can you live up to those names?"

Once again looking at each other, yet this time confused, we notice your demeanor shift. As I begin to ponder, so does my friend, and we all seem to want the same thing here.

"There's only one way to find out, love. Are you willing to test that theory?" I mention, living up to the name I was given.

You look over at Zeus, awaiting his response, but it's already been given to you as he raises his shirt, exposing his body to you.

"I like the way y'all play, but I know that y'all aren't serious."

"You don't know us well then, love. The ball is in your court. We're game if this is what you truly want to do," I assure you.

Without hesitation, you motion for the bartender. The two of us take care of the tab as you take out your phone and call for an Uber. We head outside together, waiting on the ride. Patrons look at us, mumbling things amongst themselves, but nothing seems to detour the path that we're about to head down.

"I can't believe that I'm about to do this," you state as the Uber pulls up in front of us.

"Hey love, if you aren't comfortable, you got time to back out now," Zeus states.

His voice does something to you as all hesitation leaves your mind.

"This is what I want. Let's go."

The three of us enter the Uber with the two of us sitting on the side, with you in the middle.

"How old are y'all?" you question.

"I'm twenty-three," Zeus states.

"I'm twenty-five."

"Oh, my goodness. Y'all are fucking babies out here. I'm older than both of y'all combined."

The Uber driver looks in the rearview mirror at you, throwing us an assist.

"You don't look a day over twenty-one. Enjoy yourself," the driver states.

"He's right. It's only a problem if you make it one," I mention.

Taking my hand and placing it beneath your chin, I turn your head to face me and kiss you gently. Without a second thought, Zeus does the same, leaving a smile on your face and fluid running between your thighs. You place your hand on both of our laps to get a feel of what you are about to get into.

"MMMMM," you exclaim, turning to look at us one at a time. "This is going to be fun."

The Uber approaches your apartment complex, and you

waste no time ushering us out. Your excitement is pleasing to see.

"Let's go, fellas. I don't want to waste this time or opportunity. I'm a little bit older, so one minute, I could be in the mood and the next, I'm not. I don't want to miss this window."

As the three of us enter your apartment, you toss your keys on the wooden dining room table, wasting no time in getting down to business. As Zeus and I enter, the aroma of Japanese Cherry Blossom smack us in the face. The art on the wall screams seduction, yet the ambiance in the house screams peace, alignment, and centeredness. You strip down to nothing, but your lingerie, which to our surprise, was beneath your club attire.

"Are you boys going to join me or just stand there and stare? I know I look good for my age, but auntie needs this transfer of energy."

Looking at one another, my best friend and I undress as well, joining you. You walk over to us, admiring our physiques by tracing the tattoos on my abdomen while caressing his six pack with your fingertips.

"Auntie likes. Auntie definitely likes," you mention as you work down and grope both of our genitals. "Drop them, drop them now."

As you command, we do. Both of our boxer briefs hit the floor simultaneously as you caress our manhood. Starting with me first, you drop to your knees and take me into your mouth, gently biting my shaft before sucking me in like a vacuum does dirt.

"Shit," I sigh out, looking down at you as you lock eyes with my best friend, stroking his dick.

"Aye bruh, she like that for real... Fuck," I mention to him as you bob your head back and forth with saliva dripping from your mouth onto my dick.

As you ease up on me, your attention turns to him. You waste no time slurping him up into your mouth.

"Ooooh shit," he sighs out, getting to experience the shit that I just got to experience. As you work your magic on his dick, I walk around the back of you. Lifting you up to place your body at a ninety-degree angle, your pussy is already primed and ready for war, but I decide to service you as you've serviced us, allowing my long, thick tongue to pierce you by sliding the tip of it like a credit card between the lips of your pussy, tasting the sweetness that you've acquired at the thought of us. You let out a vicious moan before reaching back to spread your ass cheeks.

"You see that, bruh? She like that shit, homie," I mention, looking up at Zeus.

"She like that shit a lot, bro, give it to her again."

After making you moan a couple more times, it was time to make you do way more than that. Stroking my dick up to its flying altitude, I slide the tip of it in you. I watch you slap the arm rest of the couch with one hand as you scratch the torso of my friend with the other. With ease, I slide my curved dick into you and begin digging into the corners of your pussy. Your pussy feels like wet velvet as I work my stroke. You feel like what I would expect heaven to feel like.

Noticing the enjoyment you're having and the reaction that it gives you, I work your pussy better so that you suck Zeus better.

"Kill her shit, bruh," he stated, wanting to push you to a limit that you haven't had before. I place one of my hands on your lower back, forcing you to arch more as you stand in front of me. My other hand grips one of your ass cheeks, as I insert my thumb into your ass.

"Oh, shit!" you cry out, losing your momentum as you feel all three holes being filled.

"Beat her mouth up, nigga, I got this."

I watch my best friend reposition his stance as he holds your head in place, stroking his dick in and out of your mouth. The constant pressure from our mannerisms has the veins in your head poking out. We're stressing and stretching you out in a way that you've been missing. You don't know which feels more pleasurable, his dick in your throat or my dick against your cervix. Your body is under a pleasurable torture, and it's on the verge of exploding.

The two of us reach up into the air, locking hands like kids used to, playing the London Bridge is Falling Down game. You begin throwing your ass back onto me and with every thrust, I meet you at your power threshold, forcing your body back forward to take his dick down your throat. The harder you toss your ass back, the harder I pump my dick into you.

"I'm cumming… Fuck, it's there, I'M CUMMING," you attempt to scream out without gagging on a mouthful of dick.

As expected, your pussy ejects my dick, and your juices run out of you like an unclogged drainpipe.

"That shit like that, bruh?" my friend questions in reference to the way your pussy feels.

"It's like that, bro, let's switch."

Our constant banter of how good you are to us, keeps you excited. The constant conversation hypes you up and gives you the feeling that just as much as you're enjoying this experience, we are as well. The two of us tag each other's hands like we were wrestlers in the WWE.

"You good, queen?" Zeus asks as he walks around behind you.

You're stuck in euphoria and can't say any words; you just toss your hand up, gasping for air. As he sits down on your couch, he pulls you over to him, sitting you down on his dick. Upon his entrance, his dick spreads your lips wider. You slap the cushions of the couch as you feel him slide deeper in you, stretching your fibers with his girth.

"Fuck!" you yell out.

He leans his head back, enjoying the feel of you, before pushing you forward. Wasting no time, I walk over and slap my dick against your face. You look up at me and smile as you take control and take me into your grasp. With both hands, you begin to stroke my dick into your mouth as you suckle the head. Within moments, you find a pace and groove to please us both and begin riding him like mad woman.

"Fuck, girl!" he yells as he dribbles your ass like a basketball on his dick. "You gone make me nut."

The pressure that he was feeling on the back end was the same that I was feeling on the front end. Before we knew it, the both of us have filled your holes with enough semen to fill a sperm bank.

You removed his dick from you and swallow the load that I've put in your mouth before falling to the floor on all fours, exhausted.

"You young niggas are bad for my health, but I love your energy. We need to make this a recurring thing."

You crawl over to your purse, pulling out a wad of money and your cell phone.

"Put both numbers in here and answer me when I call. I always want both of you, every time. Is that understood?"

In unison, he and I agree. I place both numbers in your phone as you hand the stack of money to Zeus before pointing towards the door for us to leave. We gather our belongings, walk over to kiss your head goodnight, and head for the door.

Once outside, far removed from your front door, we both

stand in disbelief at the way things have played out in our favor. We share a moment of laughter as I reach into my pocket to take a picture of your apartment number, posting it to my Snapchat story, captioning the picture *Heaven on Earth*.

"Bruh, we got a sugar mama," Zeus states, looking at the money.

"Nigga, we got a fucking sugar mama. let's keep her ass pleased," I rebut.

"You already know, my nigga. I'm down with you. I'm my brother's keeper for life."

Chapter 9

Fucking With Money

The elevator ascends us to your penthouse condo as I look at you in the reflection of the glass. You stand there, matching my fly from head to toe with your clothing. As the elevator comes to a halt, we enter after making another successful day of runs. Your drive and energy always has countered mine, which is why we work well together. You are truly my rider.

"Let's count this shit up before we put it away. I need to know where we stand," I mention to you, walking the duffle bags into your bedroom where the safes are.

Entering your bedroom, we both open the duffle bags, that are filled with cash, on the bed. As the money spreads across the bed spread, both of our eyes light up. It's yet another instance where we match one another.

"I think today was a good day," you mention, watching money slide onto the floor.

I shake my head in agreement as you take a handful and toss it in the air. Having a seat on the bed, I take a handful and begin the count.

"One, two, three, four, five, six, seven, eight, nine, one thousand."

As I thumb through hundred after hundred, you decide to wait before you begin.

"I'm going to change before we get too deep into this. It's going to take us some time to count all of this up."

I shake my head in agreeance and watch you walk to your closet. I grab another handful of money and begin to repeat the process of counting the one-hundred-dollar bills, one after another.

As you return to the room in your boy shorts and sports bra, it catches me off guard. The tomboy in you has never intrigued me, yet seeing you in your home, relaxed in your element catches my eye. I cough, clearing my throat, not wanting to make myself obvious.

"You ok?" you question, noticing that my cough has thrown me off from counting.

"Yeah, I'm good."

I recapture my focus as you join in and start counting money along with me. As we get a quarter of the way into the count, your body starts to tense up. Lifting your head towards the ceiling, you roll your neck.

"You aight?" I question this time.

"Yeah, I'm just a little bit tight."

You place one of your hands onto your back, attempting to stretch out the area that's hurting you. As you do, your perfectly formed breasts begin an attempt to escape the bottom of your sports bra. I try not to make myself look obvious watching you, but it's hard not to. Seeing you outside of normal clothes is a sight to see for any man.

"Do you think you could rub my back and shoulders right here?" you question, pointing towards the area in question.

"I got you." I place the money in my hand back into the pile on the bed and around to where you're sitting.

Standing behind you, I begin to gently apply pressure to the spot.

"Mmm," you moan out slightly, and it sounds so seductive.

I can feel a sensation inside of me as I fight to not allow myself to look at you in that way.

"Harder, please," you mumble.

As I increase the amount of pressure that I'm putting on you, your moans intensify.

"That's it, right there. Don't stop."

The urge to hide my slowly growing erection is becoming less and less important to me as you're making it hard for me to keep this at just a massage. You adjust your posture and throw your hair over one of your shoulders before reaching back and grabbing my hand for me to stop. You move my hand from your back to your neck and look up at me.

"I got something else that I need you to massage. Squeeze right here."

You have me choke you as you let out moan through a slight laugh.

"Don't be so gentle; you can't hurt me."

Looking down at you biting your lip, I apply more pressure to the sides of your throat, not attempting to hurt you, but just slightly, giving you the thrill that you're seeking. You reach out once you've had enough, tapping my arm for me to release you. You gently pull the same arm, forcing me forward, feeling my dick graze your back.

"Shit," you mention, feeling me against your back.

"I'm so sorry. I wasn't trying to have you notice that. I'll be right back."

I walk away from you and head into your bathroom to attempt to get mind, body, and spirit together.

"Come on, dawg, get it together."

After a few minutes in the bathroom, I return to your bedroom, where I notice you laid out over the pile of money.

"What are you doing?" I question.

"Hopefully crossing one of my fantasies off my bucket list. Are you down?"

With a smirk on my face, I second guess my optimism. We're too close to let anything come between us. Far too many times, we've both seen friends go down this road and never return, but I decline all thought of reason and entertain your fantasy.

"I don't think you're ready for this pressure yet," I state to you, drawing near you.

You're confident in your abilities, and you know what you want as you grab my dick, looking into my eyes.

"Yes, I am. One on one, right now, teacher to student, no interruptions, and no business. Just us."

You take both phones from my pocket and toss them into the duffle bags on the floor before kicking the bag across the room.

"Your girl will be ok for the night." I looked at you confused.

"Don't ask me how I know. You left your phone unlocked in the car while we were making a run one day, and I saw it all. She seems nice. She cares for you and your well-being. You deserve that peace in your life, but right here, right now, in this moment, I have to take care of me before you get serious enough to replace me with her in our operation."

I can't really say much to you. As a woman, you know exactly what you're doing and what it is you want. There's no running from reality, and you're content with the situation. You begin to untie my jogging pants and slide my dick out of my boxers.

"Damn, I been waiting to meet you for some time now," you state as my dick bounces upon its removal of my boxers.

Taking the head into your mouth, you begin to kiss it. I stand at the edge of the bed, watching you bob back and forth like a woodpecker on my dick. I place my hand in the middle of your thick hair and slow your pace down. You have my dick so hard right now, I feel like I could fuck through a brick wall. As I grip your hair, pulling your head away from me, I forcefully toss you back on the bed. Removing my shirt, I regroup before preparing myself to please you. Starting at your ankle, I begin slowly gliding my hand upwards over your skin. Staring into your eyes, I slide your boy shorts to the side, before sliding both my middle and ring finger into you.

"Got Damn," I bark. Words can't express how silky smooth your pussy feels. You told no lies when you said that this was what you wanted. Proceeding to remove the boy shorts from your short, thick, chocolate frame, I put your body into the position I want you. I run my fingers across your lips so that you can taste yourself before kissing your lips to do the same. Without warning, our kiss leads to me sliding my rock-hard dick into you.

"Damn, girl."

I could already feel the nut in my dick begin to run through my veins, and we aren't even five minutes in yet. Immediately, I pull out to regroup.

"What's wrong, daddy?" you question deviously. "You can't hang with your understudy?"

With a smirk on my face, I reply, "Nothing." I get my shit together before slapping my dick against your pussy before diving back in. Your pussy has the heat of an oven, the texture of honey, and is tighter than security at Fort Knox.

I ease my dick back into you and watch as your facial expressions change from devious to joyous. I begin stroking your pussy, but I know that I won't last long in the current position we're in. Readjusting the both of us, I take your legs and fold them up with your feet up by your head.

Your flexibility isn't a problem. After all, you're a former gymnast. I find comfort in this position because I can perform like you need me to. Pulling your body closer to the edge of the bed, I start digging deeper into your pussy.

"Harder," you cry out as you begin to feel my dick thrust against your walls. "That's it, daddy. Fuck me," you beg as I watch your toes slightly curl by your head.

My testicles slap against your asshole as your nectar is in full retreat mode, attempting to escape your pussy. You're so wet, I feel my torso getting drowned in your wetness. My dick is getting anxious with each moment. I begin to thrust harder, deeper, and faster into you as I stand straight up in your pussy, forcing my dick into you until I'm balls deep and lost in your abyss. You quickly shift your body, and your legs snap back into place like a bed spring.

"Too deep, daddy. Fuck! Too deep," you cry with pain in your voice.

"I thought you were ready for this pressure," I say jokingly.

Easing my dick back out of you to let you regroup, you sway your legs back and forth, trying to get your pussy to relax. I pull you closer to me while motioning for you to stand up.

"Turn around," I demand. You do as I instruct. "Lay your chest on the bed."

Although you're still feeling my dick throbbing in you from the depth of my previous stroke, you look back at me with a smile and comply. You clench your hands into the covers while I massage your pussy, just to numb the sensation. I place my hands on your waist then jam my dick back into your oozing pussy.

"Oh, fuck!" you scream out as your words get drowned out in the mattress. I begin pulling your body back onto my dick with my hands grasping your hair. Thrusting my pelvis harder into you as you submerge your head into the covers, biting them, your chilling screams become long moans as you begin squirting all over me. You buck and scream like a horse that's been violated as your pussy forces my dick out of you. I watch as it begins to drain like a waterfall onto the sheets. I gently lean over and kiss your back as I relieve myself by massaging the nut out of my dick onto your ass cheeks.

"Thank you," you mention, sighing out with a mouth full of cover. I fall onto the bed and lay next to you.

"You good?" I question.

"Fuck yes, I'm better than good now. That shit was better than I envisioned in my fantasy."

As we lay in the bed with money stuck to our bodies, you lay in my arms as we doze off with the city's skyline painted perfectly in the backdrop of the condo's open windows.

Chapter 10

Rhythm of the Heart

The two of us are both drunk after returning to your hotel suite from the Trap Lounge night club. Dealing with the traumas of life, the stars have aligned and brought us both here together this evening. We've spent most of the night getting to know one another and the issues that we're currently facing. There's one thing that's apparent, and that's the strong chemistry between us. Even if it isn't the liquor playing tricks on us, it's enough to make us believe that it's true.

Heading into the living room section of the suite, you break the ice, pushing our conversation further.

"Let me ease your pain," you state, looking at me while taking a sip from your glass.

The liquor is speaking for you, yet saying every word that we both want, and need, to hear. Placing your hands on my shoulders and back, you pull me closer to you.

"Why are you so fucking sexy?" you question, locking your fingers in into my dreadlocks, placing a kiss upon my lips, leaving the both of us stuck, standing in a trance of euphoric bliss.

Your lips taste just like Hennessy Pure White and the honey surrounding the rim of the glass.

"Damn, I want you right here, right now," you utter.

Wrapping your arms around me, you hug me, placing your

ears against my chest, dancing in place, listening to it beat at a steady pace.

"That's how I want to be stroked. Just like that. Boom, boom… boom, boom. I want the stroke constant, repetitive."

Your touch is gentle as you run your fingers over my six-foot, four-inch frame. You've done enough and got me ready to meet you halfway as I look down at you, preparing to share a kiss with you once more.

"You open to acts of service?" I question.

You look at me, confused, not fully grasping the magnitude of the question. "Fuck whether you are or not. You only live once. Let's have some fun. Strip down."

As expected, you do as you're asked and stand, watching my every movement in your bra and panties. I walk away from you, heading into the kitchenette, grabbing the ice bucket out of the mini fridge, along with the bottle of honey that we used for the rim of our drinks.

"Where are you going?" you ask.

The question is irrelevant as I return before you could finish it. Placing the ice bucket onto the coffee table, I sit you down on the sofa. Slowly, I begin to ease your panties off and kiss your inner thigh. Laying you back, I take the bottle of honey and pour it over your stomach, down your thighs, working a trail back up to your shaven pussy, marking it with an X. Reaching into the bucket of ice, I pull a piece out of it. Taking the ice in my mouth, I warm it up just enough to get water droplets to form.

With the ice in my mouth, I use my tongue and begin to follow the path I've created on your body like a treasure map.

"I promise, I won't bite. Brace yourself."

As I work up and down the trail, clearing the sticky substance from you with my tongue, I finally land at my mark.

"X marks the spot, right?"

Rotating the cold ice and my warm tongue across your clit, you allow the sensation take over. I can see the goose bumps begin to form over your skin as the ice begins to melt. I take my hands and open the entrance to your pussy, forcing my long, thick, pink tongue into your nestled cave. Grabbing the honey, I pour some more over her vaginal area, massaging it onto your pussy lips before I French kiss them passionately.

You have no words at all for what is transpiring, nor do you need them.

The way your thighs are shaking and your stomach is contracting into your back lets me know that I'm on the right path. You begin to make noises that I hadn't heard in a long time, driving me to quench my thirst of you more.

Can I make love, love, love, love, love to you. Can I make love, love, love, and show you how I do? Can I put it in ya life and give it to you right? You've been all alone but daddy's here tonight. Can I make love to you?

I begin singing to you, reciting every word of "Can I" by Tank, rotating between full words and muffled ones as I suck your pussy between words.

With one of your hands on the back of my head, gripping my dreadlocks, the other grips your own breast. You arch your back because you're on the verge of having one of the greatest orgasms of your life. I look up at you, watching how you react to the way that I've taken control. You release your body, allowing me to use your pussy as I see fit.

Suckling on your clit, craving the juices that you're about to release, I slide two fingers into you, stroking quickly.

Your moaning becomes sporadic, and you begin to lose your composure, trying to jerk away from me. Your running is not allowed as I take my arms and clamp down on your thighs, holding you in place.

Squeezing your breast tighter, you let out an aggressive, whimpered cry. Before you realize it, you've filled my mouth with your sweet flowing cum. Like a never-ending river, you drain out continuously.

I pull you down onto the floor, laying you on your side with your ass facing me. Wrapping one of my arms around you, I place one of your legs up onto the sofa and guide my dick into you.

You reach around the two of us, placing your hand on my ass, pushing me into you. Acting upon your request, I do exactly as you wish, pumping my dick into you at the desired tempo—slow, steady, and deep enough to make your toes curl with every stroke.

"Please, don't stop."

I begin to grind inside you clockwise, before reversing my pivot and grinding counterclockwise.

"Make me cum for you, please," you insist as I switch it up once again, returning to the rhythm of my heart's beat. After minutes of nothing but pressure-applied strokes, the two of us reach our climax together. Like two puppies in the summer's heat, we remain here, on the floor panting, attempting to regain our composure.

Chapter 11

Fire and Desire

"What is it about me that turns you on the most? What is your infatuation with me?" you ask in a rather sadistic tone as you attempt to massage the knots from my neck and back. Digging your pink fingernails into my skin, you tilt my head to the side, awaiting my answer.

Slightly turning my head, I manage to look over my shoulder at you as you work your hands over me.

"Of all the questions for you to ask, that's the one that came to your mind?"

"Yes," you reply gently.

Exhaling a deep breath, I formulate my thoughts to satisfy you.

"That's neither simple nor a complex answer. I'm a simple man, yet, I'm very passionate about my endeavors, if you will."

You continue canvasing my shoulders, neck, and back as if it were a portrait that you're finger painting, unimpressed by my subtle response.

"Well, are you going to continue?" you mention, clearing your throat.

Gently interrupting the massage, I take one of your hands and slowly pull it towards my mouth. With a gentle kiss to your hand, I have you.

"I'm not a man of many words, love, but actions… Actions, I do very well."

I maneuver my body in such a manner that I am face to face with you. Placing both of your arms around my neck so that you can feel my presence, I need you to feel the warmth of both my body and the desire in every exhale of my breath.

"What are you doing?" you question, caught off guard, yet intrigued with curiosity.

"I'm answering your question without words." Gently placing my lips against your neck, I clench a handful of your hair into my hands. "Most men are too afraid to show you what they want to tell you. I, on the other hand, am not. On the contrary, everything that I want to say, I'm going to do to you so that there's no confusion. Like right now. I'm about to give your body an electric shock with no electricity."

Circling my tongue over your neck, I give it a gentle bite, before sucking on the exact spot.

"Wait," you exclaim through a distressing gasp, digging your nails into my back from the sensation. "Shit," you mouthed through silence. "What the fuck was that? What are you about to do to me?"

Wrapping one of my arms around you, I stand to my feet with you suspended in the air, holding on to me by the strength of your arms alone. I place you down in the same spot that I'd just gotten up from. Clapping my hands, the mood in the room changes. In the blink of an eye, it goes from dimly lit to a deep, red glow like the transition on a silhouette challenge.

"What is my deepest desire?" I slowly sputter, removing my shirt before you. Reaching out, I take one of your hands and place it over the throbbing bulge in my Nike sweats. The gentle feel of your hands ignite a fire inside me that wants to be unleashed.

You slowly begin rubbing up and down, biting your bottom lip. I place your other hand between my chest and torso, allowing you to strum my muscular abdomen.

"Is this what you desire?" you question, placing my firm manhood into your mouth through the sweats.

I exhale a deep breath and smirk, looking down into your eyes as you look back up into mine.

"This is not my desire. It's yours," I mention, placing my hand on the back of your head, removing myself from your mouth. I can feel the curve of your lips as you smile and reach to remove my dick from its coverage.

"Tsk...Tsk...," I hiss as I take back control of the situation. "Close your eyes."

You do as requested, and the fun begins. I take my bandana and cover your eyes. I wave my hand over your eyes to ensure that you can't see anything. I pace over to my dresser, grabbing the wand massager that you've brought with you, along with an anal plug and a feather. As I return to you, your breathing pattern lets me know that you're anxious. I take your hand, open it, and place the anal plug in it.

"What's this?" you question, feeling the texture of it.

"Shhhhh… it'll all make sense in due time. Stand up."

As you do, I begin to remove your clothing from you. You stand before me naked, vulnerable, yet perfect. I take the feather, running it across your neck, across your chest until I get to your breasts. As I watch the small bumps around your areolas come to a head from the feel, I circle your nipples with it, allowing the feather's gentle feel to tease you.

"Spread your legs," I whisper into your ear.

Once again obeying me, you do it. I take the anal plug from

your hands and guide it to your mouth.

"Suck on it," I command.

You do so, lubricating it, before I take it away from you.

"Spread yourself."

Hesitantly, you do so, before letting out a rather uncomfortable sigh. You feel the plug enter you and attempt to adjust to its awkwardness inside you.

"Are you ok?" I ask, noticing your breathing pattern.

"Yes," you reply, asking me to continue.

I stand behind you, still clothed, with my dick pressing against the anal plug. I take the wand massager, placing the setting on low before placing it over your pussy. Through airy whispers and kissing on the side of your neck, I begin to answer your question.

"You see, my infatuation with you is simply this. You don't ask questions; you allow me to lead you without the fear of the unknown. My desire is you, pleasing you, the thought of you, the simple essence of you. You embody everything that a man wants in a partner. Granted, you are submissive; you are strong in your submission. You still know how to control the things you also desire. Like the orgasm you're on the brink of."

I drop the feather to the ground and place my hand against your neck.

"Cum for me."

You're growing weak in your knees from my words and the sensation you're feeling between your legs.

"Cum... for... me..."

"Shit, I can't handle this. Please, keep talking."

I take my lips and begin kissing against your neck once

again.

"This is my desire. Seeing you in your rarest form, your ultimate beauty. Now again, I command you to cum for me."

"Ohhhh, ooooh, shit."

Just like a thief in the night, your orgasm comes, and fluids rush down your thighs. Untying the bandana from your eyes, I turn you around to look at you.

"Is that answer sufficient?" I question, holding you in my arms.

"That answer was the fire to my flame. Thank you."

Chapter 12

D.S.P.O

Desire becomes surrender. Surrender becomes power.

Power becomes obsession. My obsession becomes you.

There are very few women I've come across that can go round for round with me in the bedroom and still manage to want more. You are two of them bundled in one body. You have a motor like no other and know how to match my competitive energy when it comes to pleasing. You are low maintenance and know what you want, how you want it, and when you want it.

The two of us gain our composure after coming off one of the best sessions we've had together, and I find myself running my fingers through your hair. As I recuperate, laying on my back in the middle of my California King bed, staring at the ceiling, you lay with part of your body on me, tracing the words tattooed over my torso and begin to question the very statement sketched into my skin.

"Can I ask you a question?" you utter, breaking the sounds of our heavy breathing.

"Of course. What's up?" I respond.

Since a child, I've dreaded that question. In my mind, I expect it to be a cliche question coming my way. Like most women, I expect you to ask something to fuck up the mood by asking something like *what are we,* or *where do we go from here?* To my surprise, neither of those come from your lips. Rather, a more personal question pops out.

"What does this tattoo mean? I've always been curious but never actually asked. What possessed you to get it?" you question. "It's such an abstract thought, yet, it's intriguing."

I look down at her fingers as they continue to move over the cursive writing and clear my throat.

"What it means is a lot deeper than words can truly explain. I can attempt to explain it, but it won't make sense to you until you've had something in your life that you can attach to it. It's an expression for me to tap into my other side."

You get quiet for a minute but never allow your fingers to stop moving. I take my hand and place it over yours.

"Sometimes, things are better left unanswered," I mention, in an attempt to sway the conversation in a different direction.

"We're open with each other, are we not? So, just try to explain what it is for you."

I take a deep breath and sit up. You do the same while looking up at me. Gazing into your eyes, I can tell that your curiosity isn't leaving until you have an answer. I've known you long enough to know that you're going to press the issue until you get what you want from me.

"Sunshine, let's just let this one go. This isn't something that can be put into words."

"Nope, not going to happen. So, what is it? Something you have to show and tell," you question jokingly.

"Let it—" I utter before you interrupt.

"Don't say another word, unless it's going to be the explanation of the tattoo. I don't want to hear anything else," you state, rolling your eyes and locking your arms into one another.

"Desire, surrender, power, obsession. It means the things

that you desire, you'll surrender your time, energy, patience, and love to them. Through that surrender, you give them the power to mold you into a being you don't understand. Once that power is obtained, you become obsessed with it, unlocking an entirely new entity you've had all along; you just never understood how to tap into it. It's stupid once it's put into words, I know."

"It's not. It's actually beautiful and makes sense," you reply. "Now, how would you convey that into actions?"

I get up from the bed and walk into the kitchen. Placing both hands on the back of one of the dining chairs, I exhale deeply.

"Fuck," I mumble out in a whisper, not wanting to show you the darker sides of me, but again knowing how you'll press the issue if I don't. I have no choice. I lift the chair and head back to the bedroom, where you're confused about my abrupt disappearance. Placing the chair in front of the mirror at the foot of my bed, directly between both posts of the footboard, you look at it with further confusion.

"I asked for an answer, and you brought back a chair. What the hell?"

Walking over to my closet, I motion for you to have a seat in the chair. I reach into the top of my closet and pull out a box that's rather dusty.

"So, are you gone tell me what's up or what?" you question.

"Hush... In due time, it'll all make sense. Just sit there and hold this." Handing you a whip with nine tails, I can tell that your intrigue is becoming nervous energy.

"Don't be afraid."

I place a couple items on the bed and make my way back over to you as you sit, patiently waiting. I reach out and help you up from the seat, switching our places.

"Use it," I say to you, motioning at the whip in your hand.

"What?"

"It's a whip, use it. Hit me with it."

You're hesitant but do so gently as I grunt.

"Don't be afraid. Hit me."

You take your arm back a little further and swing with a bit more power as you connect with my chest.

"Again."

Slowly, I begin to watch you through the mirror, enjoying yourself, relieving some stress.

"Phase one is now complete. How do you feel?"

"Empowered, exhilarated."

"Go to the bed and grab whatever you'd like next."

You walk over and grab the gag ball. Examining it curiously, you bring it back, along with a set and ankle cuffs. You place the gag over my head, forcing the ball into my mouth, before locking my ankles to the legs of the chair.

There's a twitch in your eye. You pick the whip back up and begin to swing at my chest even harder. The welts that're beginning to form arouse you so much, you start to feel bad for your actions. You pause your assault against my body momentarily to tend to my wounds.

I embrace the pain; it's a part of the identity that I've adapted through the process of the phases. You've officially hit phase four of the process. Your desire through your curiosity has led you to surrendering your willingness to think rationally. The power that I've given you has led to an obsession that you don't yet realize you're enjoying. As that obsession grows, so will the monster inside you, wanting nothing more but to always be in control.

Chapter 13

Darkside of the Moon

Our situation is complicated and very complex, with the both of us being married to others. However, the fear of getting caught keeps the flame burning constantly. You and I both long for a time and a place where we can have just a little more, but until our situations are resolved, neither of us can afford to place all our eggs in one basket. As you sit behind me on your knees, embracing me with a hug, I look over my shoulder into your half-dazed, caramel eyes, watching you as you smile in lust. I'm caught up in the moment and smirk back.

"Yo' ass is a mess. What the hell am I going to do with you?" I ask, reaching behind me to grip your ass. You let out a slight gasp and gently chuckle.

As I release you from my grasp, you fall back freely on the bed. Crossing your legs for a moment, your smile gets brighter.

"Well, I mean, you can stop talking about bullshit that doesn't matter in this moment and put yo' mouth to use. That's what'll benefit both of us. I know yo' fine ass is hungry, so come on and eat this buffet. Put them beautiful lips to work the right way. I know that's one reason you came over here, not to ask a bunch of questions that'll work my nerves."

Standing to my feet, I turn to admire your plush body as you spread your legs, playfully pointing towards your pussy. Bending over, placing both of my hands on the bed next to you, I gently place a kiss on your inner thigh, moving my tongue inward like a snake slithering across the grass until I reach her clit. Using my lips, I gently strum them together with your pearl between them. I slowly circle it while it throbs against my tongue. The pulse in your throbbing clit matches your heartbeat, in sync, playing the same tone.

As I go to town eating you like my last meal, you place your hands on the back of my head, winding your hips the opposite direction of my tongue's rotation, maximizing the effect of our cause.

The midnight hour has come as the clock strikes twelve, and the sins of the previous day refresh themselves, leaving the past exactly where it needs to be, giving you and me a clean slate. As we enjoy one another, the time flows as swiftly as we do, flipping through positions, exchanging orgasms, as we spend late hours of one day and the early hours of the next pleasing one another. The words of my ancestors echo in the back of my head, and they couldn't have been more right.

"Nothing good comes after midnight, and the only people out at that time are either looking for trouble or are the devil himself."

Nothing about what we're doing is pleasant in the eyes of the righteous, yet the lustful game that we're playing has me delivering the devil's dick to one of the devil's advocates, and the two of us are loving every single sinful moment.

As we rotate into yet another position for the night, you climb on top and look into my eyes, slowing down the pace in what has been a heavyweight bout between the two of us. You reach down, take your hand, and grip my dick, ensuring that it won't lose its power. You lean over and kiss my lips, before easing the curve of my dick back into you.

Knowing that morning is approaching swiftly and your spouse will be home from work soon, you fight for this moment, knowing that reality comes at six.

"I really wish you could stay all night with me. It would make everything so much better, almost perfect even." With a tear in your eye, you begin to ride my dick with passion, knowing that it can't happen.

"We both know that can't happen for various reasons," I respond, attempting to turn my head away from looking into your teary eyes. It's to no avail as you take ahold of my face, forcing me to give you a piece of me that I haven't tapped into with you before. I looked into your puppy dog eyes, biting my bottom lip, fighting back a tear myself because I long for the same things you do.

Slowly, you rotate your hips, squeezing my dick with your love muscle, continuing to live in the right now.

"Please, baby," you beg in a whispered tone as you hug onto me, damn near entering my skin.

Wrapping my arms around your body, embracing you like you're a scared child, I match your motions and emotions with my own. I place my forehead against yours and in that moment, I feel my dick losing control. Knowing that if I tap out first, I'm going to fall right into the trap you want me to. I can't stay the night here with you, I just can't.

I make a move and keep your body in position as I lift the two of us from the bed, into an upright standing position. With you suspended around me, I carry you over, towards the massive window in your bedroom. There's a ledge located at the base right before the window, in which the moon's light pierces through it.

"Wrap your arms around my neck, don't let go," I say to you.

I pull open the curtains of the window before turning to sit down on the ledge.

"If you gone ride me, do it the right way. I want to see you in the dark of the night—vulnerable, flaws and all— as the moon reflects against your skin. I want you to bring the light out of this darkness we've created. I don't want you to hide any blemish or any insecurity. I want you as naked as the night sky when the moon exposes the secrets of the dark."

Gripping your waist, I begin to pace you the way that I want you on my dick.

"I need to see the light of the night burn in your eyes when you cum for me."

We share an intimate kiss as you, too, are on the verge of reaching ecstasy. I tilt your head to the side and kiss your neck as you approach your peak.

Your bouncing becomes consistent, as I lean back, watching your breasts jump.

"That's it, baby, let me have it. Let me see that shift in your eyes while you cum on this dick. Get that nut off on this dick, baby."

Just as you're about to kick into overdrive, your pussy relaxes, allowing more of my dick to penetrate you deeper.

You scream as you reach your climax and I let out a massive growl.

The door swings open, and your husband is standing, looking at the two of us, huffing like animals.

"You raggedy ass bitch!" he yells out while rushing towards us.

The morning didn't have to come for our lives to change forever, but I want you to know that there are no regrets in the time we spent, with the decisions we made, or the games we played.

<h1 style="text-align:center">Chapter 14</h1>

Lunch Break Lover

I stand ten toes down behind you as you begin prepping dinner for the evening. I gently allow my fingertips to trace the tattoo on your lower back, raising the hairs on your neck.

"Chill, baby," you weep, getting weak from me touching your spot.

"Can I have you?" I ask in a deep, low baritone whisper, placing my fingers inside the trim of your panties.

"Baby, come on; I'm trying to prep for dinner."

"Dinner can wait. I'm hungry now."

Turning you around, I pull the spaghetti straps of your shirt down to expose your C cup breasts. I ease one of them into my mouth and twirl my tongue around your nipples, giving you a slight preview of what's to come for your clit. Pushing the chopping board with all of the colorful vegetables to the side, I lift you up onto the counter.

"Don't hurt me. Be gentle," you sigh out as you place a kiss on my lips softly.

I feel your throat contract as you swallow the remainder of your words prior to giving them life.

"Have your way," you plead.

Opening your legs, I can see that you're already dampened

from the slightest foreplay. I pull your PINK panties down from your waist and place a slap on both of your inner thighs. Holding both of your legs up, I take the tip of my long, thick, wide, tongue, rapidly working it in a motion comparable to your rose toy, allowing it to barely tease the nerves of her clit. Your juices run down to your ass, and I'm so invested in pleasing you that I catch them before they hit the countertop.

"You let out a vigorous sigh as it's a first in our relationship.

Noticing the difference in your moans, I circle the rim of your ass once again, hearing you moan louder.

What the fuck? I think to myself as I continue the process. I let go of one of your legs and begin gently working your clit. Curiously, I insert the tip of my tongue into your ass to see if I get the same reaction I do when I enter your pussy.

Moving from hole to hole, I moan over both, allowing the bass from my voice to work as a vibrating tool.

"Shit... you motherfucker," you moan, enjoying this newfound sensation you're having. "Fuck, Zaddy, I can't hold it anymore."

"You said be gentle. Now let me have it, baby. Fuck my tongue."

If I was ever thirsty, you're surely quenching it with your assault on my tongue. A couple minutes pass, and you lose all control, squeezing your breasts, which forces more fluids to drain from you. You work your hips up and down, forcing the cum to rain down. Before I can brace myself, you're flooding my beard, exhaling a vicious screech of pleasure.

Opening my mouth, I'm there to catch everything that drains out from you. You shiver on the counter but are able to clamp your legs down on my head. You come back to reality, and as any real nigga should, I put my tongue back to work and make you double up for Zaddy.

Chapter 15

Happy Endings

"Welcome to Touched by Teddy. I'll be your masseuse today. How can I please you?"

Introducing myself to you as you enter my establishment, I can tell by the smile on your face that you're excited for your hands-on experience.

"Teddy, is it?" you ask jokingly, noticing the sign on the wall. "That's a fitting name for a man who looks like a giant teddy bear."

Escorting you towards the table in the dimly lit room, you begin removing your coat, revealing a voluptuous body beneath, with very few garments of clothing attached to it.

As I help you onto the table, I begin my spill as I do with every customer.

"So, Miss, if you don't mind me asking, how did you hear about us?"

You give me a slight smirk while sitting on the edge of the table. You examine the room, glancing at the art on the wall and some of the books on the shelf. One, in particular, catches your eye as you break your silence.

"The Art of Seduction. It's one of my favorites," you mention as you continue looking around the room, noticing the different massage oils. "As for your question, well, word travels fast when the services rendered are exceptional. So, I had to come see for myself what all the hype was about. Besides, every woman deserves a good massage, does she not?"

"Every woman most definitely does," I respond.

"So far, I see nothing to be alarmed by, so what sets you apart from other masseuses?" you question.

Slightly confused, I attempt to answer your question as best as I can.

"I can't speak on others, but my experience is one of one. Once you leave here, you'll have a lasting impression of not only my facility, but a memory of your experience as well.

"Is that the spill you give all your clients, or are you really about to make me go through the hoops with you right now? You know why I'm here."

As you look into my eyes, I give you a slight smirk, knowing exactly what services you've come in search of. Walking over to the door, I lock it to ensure that none of my colleagues come to interrupt, before proceeding to turn out every light in the room. I make my way back over to you in the dark, with only the change in your breathing pattern to guide me.

"If that is your desire, your wish is your command, but before we get started, I need to hear you say it."

"Need me to say what?" you question nervously.

"Don't play with me. You and I both know why you came. Say it!"

"I don't know what you're talking about."

"If that's the case, leave," I utter, drawing closer to you.

"Ahhhh, so the Teddy bear can't handle when the roles are reversed?"

Growing rather impatient, I reach out and take a hold of your neck, gently pressing against your windpipe.

"Say it, now."

Reaching out, I feel your hand stretching down, grabbing a handful of my dick before finally breaking.

"Make me."

My grip tightens as does yours.

"Make me submit," you plead.

You've finally spat the words that I've waited for you to speak. Swiftly, I release you from my grasp.

"Good fucking girl. Now follow me."

Escorting you into the adjoining room where purple LED lights fill the ambiance, you break your silence once more. Looking around in amazement, you grow anxious, walking into *Teddy's Tabernacle.*

"So, this is what all of the hype is about? I like," you mention as you begin scanning the room, placing your hands on the different devices. "So are you as dangerous as your reputation makes you out to be?" you ask, trailing your fingers across my chest, walking circles around me.

"Dangerous?" I mocked, sarcastically laughing. "Is that something they say about me?"

The fact that you've shown no fear, no hesitation upon entering this room makes me that much more excited for what's to come. The chemistry between the two of us has you relaxed.

My voice lowers. The baritone in it carries to your ears as if it's blessed by the Gods themselves. Yet, it's as smooth as a child's bedtime melody.

"If it was, could you live up to the hype?" you press forward, seeking an answer to your question.

As you continue to circle my body, I reach out and grab one of your wrists, stopping your momentum in the process. I pull you closer to me, exhaling a gasp of air while looking into your eyes, answering you.

"I'm a lot of things, my dear, but dangerous? That's one I pride myself on being."

"Explain it to me. I want to learn," you whimper curiously.

With pleasure, I begin to explain.

"Being dangerous is a matter of perception."

I release you and turn to reach into one of the cabinets behind me, grabbing my lighter. I ignite it and allow the flame to dance before your eyes. As the glare in your eyes shift from the fire to my lips, I begin to elaborate on my stance.

"Fire is dangerous, yet, we're fascinated as humans with its beauty." Taking you by the hand, I place it above the light as it dances, allowing you to feel the warmth from the flame.

"Ouch," you utter.

"You see, from a distance, that fire is beautiful, but once you draw closer, fire by itself can hurt you."

I reach over once more, this time grabbing a candle from the top shelf of the cabinet, placing the flame to the wick. It takes merely a moment before the wick burns down enough for the candle to begin melting. Taking the wax from the candle, I pour it out over your arm.

"When combined with the right tools, that same fire can be pleasurable."

"Hmmmm." You moan out from the sensation you feel against your skin.

Taking the same arm that I've poured the wax upon, I spin

you around, admiring your physique.

"Show me more!" you beg.

I do as you ask. I hit the switch on the wall, and the motorized mount brings down a contraption over the lone table in the middle of the floor.

"Do I have your permission?" I question as you examine the different modalities of the table.

"Yes," you state without hesitation.

With your permission, we proceed, and I lay you down onto your back before strapping your legs and arms down to the table. Generally, I would blindfold my subject, but your intrigue has made me decline that option for your session.

"Relax," I state to you. "A tense nature could be harmful with the acts that are about to be performed on your body. Now welcome to the experience. Shall we begin?"

I pull essential oils from beneath the table and cover your body with them. I forcefully take my hands and massage the oils into your skin. Reaching beneath the table again, I pull out a rope, nipple clamps, and a massage gun.

I begin at your temple, rubbing it with my hands before working down your jaw line. I continue rubbing your body with slight pressure as I get to your neck, where I gently choke and caress it. I take the rope, lying it over your neck before tying it to the table.

You are pleased and want to reach out for me, but you can't because you're still restrained at both hands and ankles. As I travel down your body, I get to your breasts. I rub them gently before applying the nipple clamps.

"Shit!" you exclaim as you feel the initial pinch.

I look up into your eyes and once again ask you to relax your mind and body. I continue working down your body, releasing your negative energies out through your pores. As I get to your abdomen, I work the sides, gently applying pressure to your pressure points, causing your body to jump and react. As I reach your pelvis, I place the wand massager between your thighs, teasing your pussy.

"Fuck… Give me more please."

I oblige and reach beneath the table, pulling out a tray filled with different instruments.

"Stimulation or penetration?" I ask as I look at the options before me.

"Both," you beg once more.

Looking down at you, shocked and stunned by your answer, I remove three items. The first is a chrome set of anal beads.

"Before I proceed, are you sure?" I question, showing you the beads.

You shake your head yes as the sensation from the wand massager continues to keep you satisfied momentarily. I lift your body slightly as I insert the beads one at a time.

"Please, tell me when to stop."

Inserting bead after bead until I'm at the four one, you finally have had enough stuffed into you.

"There. No more," you respond.

I move on to the next item, which is a set of chrome kegel balls. I warm them with my hand before inserting both of them, one by one, into you. Your breaths are staggered as your pussy contracts onto them.

"Physicality or sensuality?" I ask, looking down at you with tears in your eyes. Your body is being pushed to its limit, and you have absolutely no control.

"Physicality, please."

I remove an eight-inch dildo from beneath the table, placing it between your thighs so that you're able to lubricate it before I use it on you. With one hand, I open your pussy and slide the dildo in you, feeling it tap against the kegel balls.

"Oh, my fucking gawd," you cry out.

I proceed with your massage as I find a stroke that not only applies pressure to your cervix and walls simultaneously, but I place the wand massager against your clit to ensure that your well doesn't run dry.

You are at a crossroad, fighting to breathe, scream, moan, sigh, and form thoughts. You climax repeatedly and are shivering, but that doesn't make me stop. Your massage isn't complete without the happy ending.

"Don't fight this shit. You have to relax and let go."

Not knowing what more your body could do, I push the dildo into your deeper, faster, forcing in both kegel balls as they stretch your pussy to its limit.

"Fuck you… Fuck you… Fuck you…," you scream out angrily, painfully, pleasured.

Your back arches, and your entire body is drenched in sweat beads as you lift off the table, like I'm performing an exorcism on you.

"Motherfucker… Shit…"

You begin to cry as I've tapped into the emotional side of your psyche. I remove all instruments from you and make your body go into shock again.

"That's the experience you came for. That's the difference between me and other masseuses."

You lie there, lifeless, as I watch over you, rubbing your legs, adding the finishing touches to your massage. I look down at you as you finally take a breath.

"How did you enjoy your service?" I question.

With what little energy you have left, you raise your hand, exposing your middle finger. I smile, knowing that I've performed my duty.

"That's the perfect answer to a happy ending."

Chapter 16

Lust On Sight

From the first day that I met you, I knew that you were trouble. A trouble that I'd love nothing more but to indulge in. The first time we locked eyes, I knew in that moment that you were different than the rest, and that I would have to proceed with caution.

"How you doing today? It's a pleasure to meet you," were the first words from my lips to your ears as I looked at you. From the very first time you looked up at me smiling, I knew that we were destined to be more than just friends.

Time has passed since that day, and yet, we've both silently grown fonder of one another. Neither of our pasts matter as we enjoy the right here, right now. What started as general conversation has blossomed into nothing more than me wanting to have my way with you. As the two of us sit around your apartment, enjoying one another's company, you go check to make sure that your kids are asleep before the night goes any further.

"We all good?" I question as you return.

You don't speak a word as you come sit on my lap, kissing my lips as you bypass my question.

"I'll take that as a yes," I state.

The kiss grows with passion as does the desire in my pants. You feel my dick pressing against you, and feel the urge to act.

"Somebody's happy to see me," you state, grinding against my erection. Leaning back, you dismount from my lap and drop to your knees. Surprised by both my size and girth, you smirk, and I see the twinkle in your eyes. You waste no time in grasping me into your small, but firm, hand, stroking my dick into your mouth. Even with braces, you work my dick like it's your favorite popsicle.

"Fuck," I sigh out as I feel you take me to the back of your throat, bringing tears to your eyes as you slightly gag. "That's my girl."

That one statement sends you into a frenzy as you begin to go harder. You take my hand and place it on the back of your head, wanting me to take control of your movements and I oblige. Just as I feel myself slipping away, I clench a hand full of your hair and pull you away from my dick.

Standing to my feet, I pivot our arrangement, placing you on the couch, where I just was.

Sliding your panties off, I can see the trail of wetness that your pussy has secreted from pleasing me. I get down on my knees, lifting your legs one at a time, kissing them from your toes to your ankle, up your calf, until both are on my shoulders, and my head is in between your thighs. Gently parting your lips with my tongue, I taste nothing but your sweet nectar, and it is divine. You attempt to put a pillow over your face, hiding your reactions from me, but we are well past you being shy. I toss all of the pillows from the couch, then grasp both of your wrists, forcing you to only focus on me and the way my long, thick, soft tongue works you.

I speak gently into your pussy, allowing the vibrations from my voice set in as I French kiss your clit.

"Right there, baby, keep it right there," you state as I circle around your clit like a merry-go-round.

I watch as your stomach contracts. From the looks of things, you haven't had your pussy eaten at this magnitude while being restrained in quite some time. Looking up at you as you your body begins to lose control, squirming, while you close your eyes and bite your lips, I begin sucking your pussy as I continue circling your clit.

"Come for me," I demand.

Right on cue, your back arches, and I release your hands as you grasp your nipples.

"That's my girl. That's it, baby, let it out."

As you regain your strength, my dick is as hard as steel, and I want nothing more but to be in you at the moment. You are hanging off the couch, and I get up, lifting you with me, carrying you into your bedroom. Placing you on the bed, I feel that it's only right to fuck you exactly how you'd expect me to.

Keeping you close to the edge, I take both of your legs, elevating them together. With my massive hands, I take both ankles into one hand before easing the tip of my dick into your pussy.

"Fuck," you mouth out gently as you feel an intrusion entering your body. Slowly, I work my stroke, allowing your divine nectar to spread over my dick. I can tell that you've been doing your Kegels as your pussy grips me with every stroke. As I begin to work deeper into you, I notice that your pussy is starting to grip as it creams on my dick, which leads me to believe that you're working up to another nut.

Spreading your legs so that I can watch your face, I begin to help you along on the journey.

"This dick feels good, don't it, baby?"

"Uh huh," you state, biting your bottom lip while shaking your head through a distressed moan.

"I need that nut on daddy dick, baby. Cum for me."

My stroke becomes longer, deeper, harder, as your pussy begins to receive me with an open invitation. Your sighs and moans have now become muffled screams as my hand finds its way to your throat.

"Come on this dick, pretty girl. Daddy needs you. Get that nut for me, baby girl."

Your pussy begins to pour as I continue stroking. Your orgasm is on the brink of explusion, and my pelvis is a fucking mess.

"Let it all go, baby girl."

Once again, right on cue, you open the flood gates, releasing everything that remained inside of you. I don't pull out, however, as I'm on the brink of my nut. You begin to grip my dick, milking me inside you. I fall out onto the bed next to you as you roll over and lay on my chest, running your fingers over me.

"Thank you," you state. "I needed that." With a simple kiss on your forehead, you doze off, and I do the same.

Chapter 17

Haitian Head Doctor

(HRS & HRS CHALLENGE)

As Jazmine Sullivan's "On It" echoes throughout the room, I watch you dance like a serpent across the floor towards me. My legs are tied to the chair that you've placed in the middle of the room. You've left me completely defenseless with my hands tied together behind my back with your silk hair wrap. Wanting nothing more than to feel your skin against mine, I grow impatient as the dance continues.

"Stop playing with me. Come here."

Slowly, you pace towards me. Come sit on it," I order as you work your way closer.

You walk over to me, taking a handful of my dick before dropping to your knees, looking up into my eyes and kissing the tip of it.

"Is this what you want?" I hear you question as you begin to circle it with your tongue.

With a shake of my head, I nod yes.

"I can't hear you," you mention, running your lips ever so gently over the most sensitive part.

"Yes, that's what I..."

Before I finish my statement, the warm sensation of your

throat grips my dick, forcing a moan to release from my diaphragm.

"Fuck, baby. Please don't stop."

As stubborn as you are, you look up into my eyes with a tear building in your tear ducts and drop your head back down as far as your throat will allow you to take me. Without hesitation, you come up, face soaked with the saliva from your mouth.

"I have an idea; I'll be right back," you state, walking away from me.

I hear you change the song in the background as you place it on repeat. The intro to Muni Long's "Hrs & Hrs" plays vividly as you return to your knees to please me. You hum the intro into my dick as if it were a microphone.

"Try not to nut," you state, looking up at me.

Yours, mine, ours, I could do this for hours.
Sit and talk to you for hours.

As Muni finds her groove over the beat with her lyrics, you do the same with my dick. You take both of your hands, place them over my manhood, and twist my shaft as you suck on the head. As the song gets deeper and the melody intensifies, so do your abilities. You work like a possessed soul with no regard for your own life as you refuse to come up for air.

You place me at the back of your throat, humming the chorus of the song, forcing me to lose my composure.

I can do this for hours, and hours, and hours. I could
do this for hours, and hours, and hours.

With every step of the way, you work my dick, following the lyrics of the song, only coming up for air as if you were on stage, performing it yourself. You remove me from your mouth and begin to stroke me with your hand as you break down into an outright concert with the tip of my dick.

"Usually, I don't like nobody, and when I say nobody, I mean nobody. All these niggas full of shit; you just a homie once they hit, felt like giving up on love, these niggas almost made me quit."

Then I met you, when I met you, I knew this was it, I never been in love like this.

This part of the song hits home for you as you begin to cry tears of joy, pleasing me. You return to your two-handed stroke, this time leaving just enough of your hand open to take my dick deeper in between strokes. Your face is a mess from the tears and saliva, yet you continue to work to drain me.

I'm losing myself as I beg for you to slow down, but you refuse. The pressure that's building up in my shaft is soon to blow, and you want all parts of the show as you continue singing and stroking the nut up to its final destination.

I can sit and talk to you for hours, sit and look at you for hours, making love to you for hours, laying on your chest for hours.

As Muni begins to shift into her *ohhh* melody towards the end of the song, my dick erupts into your mouth and over your hands like a geyser in the middle of northwestern Wyoming. You smile at the welcomed sight and devour every drop that's emitted from my body, squeezing my dick to ensure that nothing is left. You remain on your knees as you lay your head on my chest, listening to the rapid pace of my heart beating.

After a few moments, you sit back onto your knees, once again looking up into my eyes as they are glazed over and red. Taking my flaccid manhood into your hands, you smile.

"It looks like someone doesn't want to play anymore."

You take my dick and place the sensitive tip back into your warm mouth and talk to it as I weep, wanting a moment to regain my composure.

"It's ok, big fella. I have just the trick for you. You're lucky that I have nothing but time, and mama likes to do this shit for hours."

Chapter 18

FaceTime

It's been months since I've laid eyes on you face to face, and the distance, quite frankly, is killing me. As I spend my days and nights with nothing but hard, hairy-legged men in training camp, the moments that we do get to share talking to one another are nothing less than spectacular. Most of our time is spent telling one another how much we miss each other or how much we love one another. The rest is spent trying to make the best out of the situation, ensuring that we don't allow outside influences to come in and break what we've built. Your faithfulness and dedication to me while I'm away has always been admirable, and whatever it takes for me to keep a smile on your face, I'm willing to do. Breaking away from my team for a bit, I attempt to take advantage of the moment.

"Shhhh… Can you hear that?"

"Hear what?" you question.

"Exactly, that's the problem. It's silent. I need your moans and sighs to echo throughout this room. Go get on the bed while I turn down these lights.

"But…"

"Don't question me. I don't need you to fix your lips to say shit other than what I'm asking for. Just lay back and relax. Let me handle everything while you tell me about your day."

"Mmmmm. You are something else, boy," you reply, making

yourself comfortable.

"Take them pants off and spread them legs for daddy."

"Yes sir."

"Mmmmm. I been waiting to talk to her all day. You ready for me?"

"Yes, daddy."

As you grab ahold to your rose, you prepare for the session ahead of us. I slide my hand down into my boxers so that you can see me pleasing myself as well.

"Put my head exactly where you want me. Allow me to take the tip of my tongue and circle your pussy like a spiraling bullseye."

I watch you take ahold of your breast through your tank top as you place the rose over your clit.

"Fuck," you moan out.

I enjoy talking shit to you as you allow me to please your mental and physical from a distance. There's nothing more gratifying than knowing that I can still make you weak for me, and that the bass in my voice exponentially turns every single follicle of your being on.

"Damn, you taste exactly how I expected you to, ever so sweet. Put your hands on the back of my head and work them hips up into daddy's mouth."

I watch you grab a pillow through the screen and place it between your thighs over the rose. Your breathing pattern begins to change as you fall deeper under my spell. There's a knock on the wall and as I turn to look, I notice two fingers being held in the air. I shoo away the perpetrator and make the most of the very little time we have left.

"Baby, we ain't got much time left. I need you to give me

everything you've got. Treat this like the last time we'll ever speak. Cum for me… Don't stop until you drain every ounce of your cum for me."

You get silent for a moment, pressing the button on your rose to increase the speed of its vibration. Just as we're reaching the closing seconds of our time together, I hear you scream out.

"Oh… my…. fucking… gawd… Shit, I'm cumming…"

Watching in amazement, I stoke my dick faster, harder. I, too, join you in bliss as both of us breathe heavily.

The knock on the door comes again, and I know that our time has come to an end.

"I love you," I state.

"I love you too. Now go make mama proud. I'll be here, same time, same place tomorrow."

The FaceTime call disconnects as the memory of you cumming is etched in my memory. I exit the room and head towards the training facility with thoughts of you on my mind, only praying that I'm returned to you soon.

Chapter 19

Crucifixion

"So, what's the deal with the bars on the wall?" you ask, examining the four of them and their positioning.

I look up at the bar with a sardonic smirk on my face as I chuckle.

"Play your cards right, and you'll find out soon enough.

You turn to look back at me, noticing the energy I have in my response and smart off.

"Consider them played."

"Are you sure that this is a game you want to play with me? I'm worse than that little motherfucker SAW riding the bike," I mention, adjusting my posture by placing both hands into my pocket.

Your refusal to back down is apparent as you place your freshly manicured fingernails onto my chest.

"I asked a question, so I'm expecting an answer. Either tell me, show me, or shut up."

Taking you by the hand possessively, I look into your eyes, watching a reflection of myself in them.

"There's no coming back from this; I want you to understand that."

You take your arm back and cross them together, still

awaiting what the purpose of the bars are.

"Suit yourself," I state, removing my shirt before pushing your toned body back against the wall.

Stunned by my aggressiveness, you decide to match my force with your own by slapping me. Grabbing you by your wrist, I pin both of your arms over your head before kissing your neck. The moment is intense as you try not to allow the sensation to take over you, wanting to remain angry with me.

"Shit," I hear you utter as my tongue charts over your neck.

"Calm yo' ass down. You asked for an answer and to be shown. I'm about to give you both. Now kiss me."

The two of us engaged in a fiery kiss as I keep your hands pinned against the wall. Our tongues dance around one another's, like snakes mating. As the kiss intensifies, so does the desire in my loin.

I soon release your arms before stepping away from you. I look inside my top drawer and pull out two pairs of black and red wrist cuffs. After attaching one to each bar on the wall, I return my attention. I place my hand around your neck and watch your eyes bounce with excitement before they roll to the back of your head while you grit your teeth.

You reach out with both of your hands, digging your nails into my skin, leaving small indentations. Without hesitation, taking both arms, I reach between your legs, cradling both of her thighs, elevating you into the air. The two of us shared another kiss as I hold you, suspended in the air, pelvis to pelvis.

"Come get this pussy, daddy," you moan.

In the blink of an eye, I elevate you, placing your feet on the lower two bars, forcing you to balance on them as I lock your hands, wrists into place on the upper two.

"This is called crucifixion."

You look down at me as you're not sure what's about to happen next.

"You don't think that you should've told me that was the name of this contraption before you put me up here?"

With a devious smirk, I remove your biker shorts. It's revealing to me that you don't have any panties beneath, as I am face to face with your trimmed pussy. I reach down and lock your ankles into place.

I take my hand and run them over your face, giving you a playful, gentle slap to the face.

"You pushed this issue, remember?"

Placing my hand over your mouth, you gently suck my middle finger. I move slowly down your body, feeling its terrain before I begin removing the demons from your soul. With your legs wide open, I enter your pussy with my index and middle finger. You moan out from the first touch you've had in a while. I gently stroke my fingers into your ocean, while I pull back against your pelvic floor, as if it were waves crashing against the shore.

"Oh shit," you mumble, not expecting the feeling you're receiving.

I ease up on the penetration as I spread your lips to expose your pearl.

"Hey there, pretty girl," I mention as I extend my tongue and cuff your clit with it.

The rare ability that I have to take and fold my tongue over comes in to play as I'm able to cover your entire clit.

Gravity works against you. As I work back and forth against your clit, your thighs grow wetter by the moment. Every fluid inside of you is draining out down your legs. I can hear you struggling for freedom as the chained lock holding the wrist cuff clinks.

"What the fuck are you doing to me?" you ask.

"I'm about to take your fucking soul."

I bury my face into your pussy, suckling onto your clit, as I reenter my fingers into you. Wanting to be able to put your hands on me, you struggle to hold it together. Your breaths are labored, your stomach contracts. Before you know it, your head is facing upwards, towards the heavens as you open your mouth, releasing a silent scream. Your voice is absent as you have no control of your diaphragm.

In a matter of moments, you inhale a deep breath, and your sound returns as you release a screech that's like a siren in the open sea.

I back away from you with my mouth and beard covered in your juices. I pull out my phone and snap a picture of you as you hang your head, completely drained. I attach the photo to our OnlyFans page with the caption, *Nailed her ass to the cross.*

WANT TO INTERACT WITH T'ANN MARIE & HER TEAM? JOIN OUR READERS GROUPS ON FACEBOOK!

T'ANN MARIE PRESENTS: GRANDMA'S HOUSE | Facebook

T'ANN MARIE PRESENTS: GRANDMA'S HOUSE 2.0 | Facebook

WIN PRIZES, BE APART OF LIVE BOOK DISCUSSIONS & MORE!

Join Our Mailing List:

http://eepurl.com/gU81k5

TMP
TANN MARIE PRESENTS
is now accepting submissions in the following genres
URBAN FICTION * URBAN ROMANCE
STREET LIT * URBAN PARANORMAL
INTERRACIAL ROMANCE
for consideration, please email the first 5 chapters of your manuscript to:
TANNMARIESUBS@GMAIL.COM